Praise for *Death by Harmony*

"The writing is good, the narrative is great. This is an important book. The world just doesn't know it yet."

> — *Readers' Favorite 5-Star Review by Ray Simmons, China*

"Great book that gradually builds to a significant day. The diction is exceptional and the imagery vivid. I would highly recommend this novel."

> — *Pre-launch review*

"Fascinating, well-researched. Read it in two sittings."

> — *Joe Der, Chinese-born meteorologist*

"Quite exceptional."

> — *Tod Hoffman, formerly of the Canadian Security & Intelligence Service*

grey gecko press

Design by Grey Gecko Press

This is a work of fiction. Names, characters, businesses, places, events, locales, and incidents are either the products of the author's imagination or used in a fictitious manner. Any resemblance to actual persons, living or dead, or actual events is purely coincidental.

Published by Grey Gecko Press, Katy, Texas.

www.greygeckopress.com

Printed in the United States of America

Library of Congress Cataloging-in-Publication Data
Berger, Leon
Death by harmony / Leon Berger
Library of Congress Control Number: 2018936400
ISBN   978-1-9457605-2-5
First Edition

DEATH *by* HARMONY

Being a journal of the tumultuous events

that occurred in Beijing on Monday, March 19, 2012,

as witnessed by those directly involved

A novel by

LEON BERGER

1

That day, we could taste the air.

ZHAO 赵

The pre-dawn gusts seared his throat and choked his lungs. He needed to rid himself of the phlegm but that would be difficult if he wished to avoid disturbing the young couple who rented his spare room. His error had been in leaving the window open last night to capture the spring breeze but the early arrival of the winds was unexpected and the gap had merely served as a gateway for the swirling irritants.

Now with tinges of gray in his hair, Zhao had been raised during more difficult times and like most of his generation, he recognized that the sudden volte-face from Mao's rigid collectivism to Deng's get-rich capitalism had been a pivotal achievement by every measure except one. Before wealth, even before nutrition, comes the ability to breathe—and these days, his home city of Beijing endured the worst pollution of any major conurbation on the planet.

The main reason, as Zhao understood it, was the unrestricted use of coal-fired plants coupled with the ever-growing automotive gridlock. Yet that was not the worst of it.

Over the years, deforestation had encouraged the dry gales that ripped through the Gobi to carry cyclones of sand down toward the vast plain of the capital. Here, the harsh grit mingled with the existing contaminants, just as it did this morning, making the atmosphere thick and leaving a coating over every surface.

At one point, in a much-hyped countermeasure, the ministry announced an emergency program to plant six million new trees known locally as the "Great Green Wall" but it resulted in failure because the saplings were of the wrong species. All they did was drain the remaining water source, leaving the subsoil exhausted and the surface denuded. If anything, the situation had deteriorated, so now all the government could do was broadcast its weather alerts across every technological platform and even then, such warnings meant little. For all but the very young and the very old, this day would be no different from any other—and that included Zhao.

A freelance interpreter, he had a job to do and knew from experience that a reputation was the most precious of assets, which meant that he couldn't allow himself to be delayed. Despite his professional skills, he saw himself primarily as a worker, born in the year of the ox, and while he'd never possessed the physical characteristics of that worthy animal, he could well believe that the astrological sign had indeed affected his approach to life, which was that of a reliable but in some ways stubborn individual.

As he wiped the residue from his eyes and roused himself from his solitary cot, he heard the young people stir in the next room. They, too, were finding it hard to resist the compulsion to cough. While such tenants helped supplement Zhao's sporadic income, the amount he charged them was modest, an empathy on his part because he could well recall the time when he, too, lived in squalor, subsisting in a filth-encrusted hovel while he and his fellow undergraduates tried to keep body and soul together.

In winter, there was little produce available and the administration dumped truckloads of stale cabbages on street corners for people to pick over. It wasn't much but without that municipal charity, their conditions would have been far worse. In summer, things were always a little easier but some were still so lacking in protein that they were actually pleased to have ants invading their abode, because the insects could be trapped and cooked as extra nourishment in their weak broth.

These days, Zhao's attitude was one of fatalism, the only option that kept him sane, and with just a ritual morning sigh, he stepped into the cramped shower area in back of his minuscule kitchen. Sometimes in the drought season, they turned off the water supply without notice but he was glad to see that it was still functioning on this of all days, even if the trickle that emerged was the color of slate and the bar of soap he'd purchased the previous month was almost down to a sliver. It was important that he present himself well on this special morning.

Like many citizens, Zhao had already visited the Great Hall of the People but never during the party's National Congress, so for this occasion he'd had his white shirt laundered and his one good suit pressed. To complete the outfit and help him look like others in attendance, he would wear his red tie and attach a tiny patriotic flag to his lapel.

Once he was brushed and dressed, he sat himself down by the wooden table to finish his meager breakfast and think about his wife and daughter still up there in Changchun, the industrial city in the northern province of Jilin where he began his career. Then he tidied around as best he could, gathered the briefcase that he carried for effect and quietly descended to the street. Only then, a solitary figure in the early morning, did he allow himself to cough again, longer and more violently this time, and was thankful when he was at last able to slide into the comfort of the small German sedan that was parked right below his window.

The new vehicle was his status, his mark of achievement, even though its shine had been reduced this morning by the thin layer of sand. He'd had to compete in an auction for the right to purchase a license plate and even then, he was only authorized to use the vehicle on alternate days but that didn't diminish the fact that its acquisition had fulfilled one of his most cherished ambitions. Like five million other drivers in this city of twenty million, he felt a certain guilt knowing that the carbon monoxide spewing from his exhaust only added to the level of asphyxiation, yet he was now a proud car owner, which instantly elevated him into a more respectable class of citizen.

LIANG 梁

In Zhao's spare room, it was Liang who rose first, her sinuses and nostrils clogged, having been wakened by her own snoring. Gently, she shook her boyfriend, Chen, but all he did was reach for her, as ever. He always wanted her at first light, told her it was the most romantic time of day, but this morning there was no time. Like their landlord, Zhao, they also needed to get an early start.

First though, they would need a little breakfast, since they didn't know when they might next be able to eat. There was cold rice and some spicy vegetable stir-fry from the previous night which would have to do, along with the ubiquitous tea, a pouch of oolong that she'd brought back from her home in Hebei province on her last visit.

She'd gone back during Golden Week, the spring new year festival when it was traditional for all city dwellers to go to their villages or farms, a throng of millions moving about the country by bus, by train and more frequently these days by air, too, crowding stations and squeezing through terminals, all trying to obtain that precious time at home with their parents and cousins, all the ones who'd never left. From the metropolis they brought money and gifts, whatever they could manage, and for that one week they pretended to be paragons, the brave progeny who had ventured out into the world and made it against all the odds.

Yet more often than not, the reality was different. The jobs they claimed to have were neither as secure nor as well-paying as they intimated. Their apartments weren't quite as deluxe as they described. Even their marital situations might not be entirely truthful and it was by no means unknown for a fake girl or boy to be hired for a few days to accompany them home in order to persuade the family that all was well, that their offspring were in settled relationships and that grandchildren could be expected sometime soon, maybe after the next pay raise or the upcoming promotion.

So it was with Liang. Much to her own shame, she had taken Chen back to Hebei merely to show him off and was only employed here in Beijing as a relief teller in a state bank. This meant she only worked when someone else was sick, in which case they would call her in at a moment's notice. It wasn't a good situation but she held on to it instead of looking for a better job in the private sector for one simple reason: coming as she did from a neighboring province, she had no *hukou* within Beijing.

This was the official permit that would allow her access to the city's social amenities, everything from healthcare to education, and without it she felt helpless. If she became ill here, if she ever wanted to have children, if she ever wanted them to attend the public school system, she would need a *hukou* and the best way to get one, short of outright bribery which she could not afford, was to gain full employment at a government enterprise. That's why she stayed for two years in the same position and would probably continue to do so until she received her opportunity to advance. Once permanent, she could then apply for the precious document. It had been promised to her by a favorite supervisor but a bureaucrat's promises don't amount to much because, like everyone else, they're at the mercy of the system.

To a great extent, it was also why she lived with Chen. Although she'd taken him back to her hometown, she didn't especially love him, she knew that, but she did kind of like him, if only because he was more polite and respectful than most males she'd ever known. However, the big advantage was that he was a native of the city, which meant yet another option for the vital *hukou*—and in this society, it was on the basis of such practicalities that decisions of love and happiness were often made.

CHEN 陈

The problem for Chen was that he, too, was low on the career ladder. He'd graduated in the hope of becoming a journalist but when a solitary position opened up at the Xinhua news agency, there were over three thousand applicants. Even then, the job went to an existing editor's nephew as expected.

So, despite Chen's meritorious credentials, he was left to scratch out several articles a day for a current affairs blog and hope that he could gain a reputation. The key was to maintain a hard edge to his writing, to push his own provocative criticism while staying shy of the ever-intrusive censorship laws. There were now upward of sixty thousand inspectors policing the web, which meant that his own blog could very soon become a target for crackdown. At the pace at which he was gaining followers, it was only a matter of time before he became successful enough to matter. Until then, he wrote his digital columns, continued attending job fairs with all their meaningless interviews and worked hard at his relationship with Liang.

At least he had a girlfriend, unlike most of his friends in this increasingly unbalanced society. With only a solitary infant allowed and a low-cost prenatal way to tell the baby's gender, it was inevitable that most parents would opt for a boy. The result was a seventeen percent difference at marital age and although new laws were trying to correct that imbalance, it was too late for the current generation. Chen therefore counted himself fortunate to be with Liang, even though she might only be doing it for his resident's *hukou*. He was aware of her motivations but he understood well enough how life worked. They co-existed. They shared a bed and they fused their lives together, somehow hoping that the miracle of love might one day be generated through the zeal of ambition.

For a while longer, Chen lay back and watched Liang puttering around the tiny kitchen area with its single hotplate and cracked sink. From the small, ancient fridge which made creaking noises for most of the night, she took plastic containers and emptied the contents into bowls. But Chen also had things to do, so he dressed quickly and immediately restarted his texting from the night before, his fingers and thumbs working rapidly to send out as many last-minute messages as he could.

"How many do you think will show up today?" Liang said to him as they finally sat down to eat.

"Who knows?" he replied, reluctantly exchanging his smart phone for the crude wooden chopsticks she handed across to him. It was an impossible question to answer. This was Monday, the first sitting of the National Congress, so there might be a multitude, or there might be just a few core supporters in the square, with the rest intimidated by the expected increase in security.

"You still want to go?" she asked him.

To Chen, her voice sounded tentative and he wasn't sure if she, too, was giving way to her fears or whether she simply wanted his reassurance. "We have to go," he told her, trying to display a confidence he didn't necessarily possess.

ZHAO 赵

As Zhao drove from his home district of Laoshan toward the distant city center, the sodium streetlamps and the quartz headlights produced a strange glow through the atmosphere, each projecting its own ghostly aura which just dissolved into the surrounding smog.

At one point, not far from the Wukesong intersection, he noticed a group of young people through the haze who looked suspiciously as if they might be activists, just like his two tenants. They stood around furtively, no more than soft shadows, some wearing dual-purpose medical masks that not only helped protect their sinuses but also served to camouflage their identities.

Traffic was already in stop-go mode even at this early hour and Zhao had a chance to watch them through his windshield, to study their body language, to try to decipher how committed they really were to this course of action. He felt a certain trepidation of what it might yield. History's task, he believed, was to instill caution into such youthful enterprise, with severe consequences if the warnings were ignored—a lesson he'd learned from his own long experience.

In his early childhood, Zhao was a witness to the catastrophic upheavals when the so-called Red Guards were given official sanction to run amok with their fingered accusations and table-top tribunals. While wall posters depicted workers and soldiers with muscular arms raised in revolution, impressionable teens, no more than grown children, were given the raw power to seize their own targets and drag them off to dingy basements for inquisition, all while waving their little Mao books and chanting their repetitive slogans. These victims were invariably labeled "bourgeois" or "decadent" or "reactionary" and thousands of them were sent away on these juvenile whims, banished to the newly collectivized countryside for re-education, where they slaved in the barren fields while slowly starving to death.

After Mao's misguided attempts, the next threat happened toward the end of successor Deng's tenure, when Zhao was already well into adulthood. This time, the students were not demonstrating *for* the government but against it. Their demands were for more democracy, more openness, and while many of the first protests were scattered in areas of west Beijing, their ultimate focus became the great central square of Tiananmen, because they believed they had the moral right to challenge the government at its core.

Of course they knew the risks, spoke of them constantly, but did any of them ever think it would really happen? That the diminutive Deng, frail and grandfatherly, would ever have the temerity to call on his forces, not just the police with their water cannon, nor even the militia in riot gear, but thousands of front-line troops equipped with assault rifles and a squadron of tanks? That his standing orders would be shoot to kill, all in the name of peace and harmony?

Zhao was there that night, not as a protester but as a bystander, an interested observer, but then the shots began to ring out, echoing around the pavement and buildings. At first, he couldn't believe it was happening, that the military would fire on its own citizens. He just stood there as people around him began to duck and panic. Then he ran too, ran hard, ran for his life into the warren-like *hutongs* southwest of the Zhengyang Gate, ran until he was ready to collapse from the expense of energy, to lie down on the filthy cobbles and allow his exhausted frame some rest.

He felt his pulse pounding and his temples throbbing but he didn't move from that alley, not for hours. He didn't know how safe the streets would be, how serious would be the crackdown, so he waited until the first glimmer of daybreak and only then did he creep away.

He'd been a witness and he'd managed to escape but that didn't eradicate or even ease the initial shock. The indiscriminate killing he'd seen would eventually be hushed up, wiped from domestic memory as if it had never happened, and even now, all these years later, the globally recognized tragedy at Tiananmen would never be called a massacre within the borders of China but merely whispered from one individual to another as "the events of June 4." It had been eradicated from all written reference and remained merely anecdotal, a fragment of folklore that the authorities hoped might eventually be consigned to the status of allegory, a tale that might serve as a warning.

Did this current generation comprehend anything at all of what happened, Zhao was wondering? They were idealists after all and idealists are often naive by definition, seeing only nobility, perhaps even martyrdom, in the ardent promotion of their cause. Inevitably, they believe their suffering will make a difference, draw attention to their protestations, but that was not how life worked nor how it had ever worked.

In fact, many people had rituals to popularize their own destruction—the Buddhists of Tibet with their self-immolation, the Islamists of Xinjiang with their suicide bombs—but who remembered any of their names? Did they all think they could become icons for the millennia? The truth was that over a relatively short time, they and their actions were simply forgotten, if not by the next day, then by the next week, and certainly by the next year. As for himself, Zhao felt that he'd already seen too much needless violence and while he sincerely hoped he was no coward, he preferred to shy away from situations which required overt bravery. Perhaps some things were indeed worth the fight but to his mind, engaging in obvious risk was like volunteering for death and that was just reckless.

As he drove on, he shook his head slightly, trying to cleanse his mind. The strange light had already spread its glow over the high-rise silhouettes and he knew that his client for the day, Anders, would soon be expecting him. If he were late, neither traffic, nor protest, nor health-damaging pollution would be sufficient excuse.

2 *That day, the skies were yellow.*

ANDERS

Still deadened by trans-Pacific jet lag, Anders raised his bald head from the eider pillow and reached for a button on the bedside panel. With a low hum, the curtains began their withdrawal, followed in similar fashion by the translucent gauze of the nets, as regal an opening as any Lincoln Center production.

For a few moments, he just tried to absorb what his western blue eyes were seeing. There'd been mornings like this in a thousand such hotels all over the planet and he'd experienced weather patterns from tornados to typhoons but he'd never witnessed anything remotely like this.

Through the heavy smog he could just about make out the Central Business District with more office space than all of Manhattan but the vague skyline was not what held his gaze this morning. It was the sky, the intense yellow sky, and for some reason his weary brain was seeking an adjective to describe the color, perhaps so he could make the anecdote convincing, another traveler's tale to astonish the dinner guests back home. He thought of "radiant," then "luminescent," before settling on "fluorescent." Yes, he decided, this was nothing if not fluorescent yellow, as in comic-book yellow, science-fiction yellow. No other description came close.

It occurred to him to cancel the day's schedule in order to remain within the hotel's advanced air conditioning system which served to filter out the external toxicity. He could use the morning to catch up with correspondence, he was thinking, or to examine the revised budget consolidations that had been forwarded from New York. There were any number of major and minor functions waiting for him to complete and he contemplated a morning with his laptop, ensconced in the ground floor coffee shop. Then a quiet lunch, maybe a nap and at the end of the afternoon, a swim and a sauna. It would make for a relaxed, pleasant day, the kind he could so rarely enjoy. But of course, it was impossible. On this day, he was to be an honored guest.

His local venture partner, Huang, had spent considerable effort in arranging this special schedule and to mark the occasion, Anders had also invited his regional vice president, Tse, a Hong Kong-based woman with whom he'd once had a brief relationship. He'd even made sure to engage his longtime interpreter, Zhao, and it was now far too late to cancel any of them.

With a sigh, Anders picked himself up from the bed and wandered through to the bathroom where he unsealed the bottle of imported water in order to brush his teeth. In this, he regarded himself as neither extravagant nor obsessive but simply mindful. It was simple common sense not to use what came out of the faucet but his concern went further, refusing to use even the local product. It might look like it was sourced from the Alps, with a pink mountain label that was eerily similar to the French original, but Anders was wary of these *shanzhai* copy brands—and it was this primary caution as much as the pollution which told him he was once again back in Beijing.

TSE 谢

At twelve thousand feet, there was still a dome of blue above the layers of yellow-brown and as Tse glanced out from her business class seat, she could view the demarcation all too clearly. Descending into that atmosphere would be like diving into a bowl of her grandmother's wonton soup but it wouldn't be for a while yet. They'd already circled the airport twice and still hadn't begun a final approach.

She was wearing black today, as she invariably did on trips up to the mainland. Back at home in Hong Kong, she could wear her bright purple hoodie with the pink pants as she went for a jog around the Peak, the dog alongside, but for some reason, darker tones always seemed more appropriate in this bigger, dirtier environment. And while she'd once bleached her collar-length hair blond, she'd since reverted to her own coloring, including a natural white streak which she decided to keep as a gesture of individuality. Unsure of the style at first, she'd been complimented so many times that she now thought of it as a useful look for her, projecting the balanced image of a mature decision-maker with just a hint of contemporary flair.

Nevertheless, despite all her preparations, she was tired of so much flying across the region and wished she could have found the courage to cancel today's events. It would have meant saying no to her one-time lover, which would have been no problem at all, but since the man also happened to be her global CEO and they were due to meet one of their organization's foremost Asian associates, she felt she could hardly refuse. While lesser staff had the option of crying off such occasions, the responsibilities of senior management were an essential part of the company ethos.

At last, the captain activated the speaker system but it was only to announce that they were still awaiting approval to land due to lack of visibility. It was annoying and there were audible groans around the cabin but at least he was polite, speaking first in *putonghua*, the standard form of Chinese in which she was just about conversant, then in her parents' Cantonese dialect and lastly in her own mother tongue, English.

Like many citizens of the former British colony, her family had transferred from Hong Kong to Vancouver just before the so-called "handover" from London's control to that of Beijing. At the time, nobody knew how such change would occur, whether it would be peaceful or chaotic, and Canada had become a safe haven thanks to a fast-track economic provision in the country's immigration laws, hastily passed to welcome exactly the kind of investment prospects that her family represented. All told, it was a disruptive move for the youthful Tse but it turned out to be the making of her career and despite her place of birth, she considered herself to be fully North American in language, culture and every other way.

After showing much early promise, she was transferred to the larger London office until, with karmic irony, she was eventually asked by Anders to return to her city of origin with a mandate to run all of East Asia. Only then, only once she'd become a ranking player in her own right, was he even interested in any other way—turned on, as he once said, by her "lust for achievement." But while he definitely meant the phrase as a compliment, she was never totally sure whether to accept it as such.

Was this really what her life was all about she sometimes wondered? Making her year-end numbers to qualify for ever more vested options, then perhaps eventually a seat on the board? And if she survived all of that with her health intact, she could look forward to retirement in a house with chandeliers. It was the acceptable dream, the goal to which everyone must aspire, but for her it was all just a giant question mark because it was just so predictable. Yet here she was, still going through all the motions, not because of company commitment or even personal reward, but from some inner kinetic drive that made it simpler to continue at the same pace than to slow down or stop.

ZHAO 赵

Stalled in the endless congestion, Zhao began to feel ashamed of his own hubris. He'd been proud of his new vehicle and had chosen to indulge his sense of self-esteem but he was now paying the price, hemmed in on all sides as he tried to reach the central core.

According to the digital clock on the dashboard, he had just a quarter-hour to make his scheduled appointment and as each minute ticked by, he was becoming ever more anxious. Unfortunately, there was little he could do except call ahead and leave an apologetic message for his client at the hotel.

Around him were the older apartment blocks and blighted discount stores typical of the area, while across the street was a large construction site, fenced by a panoramic illustration of what the finished condominium project would look like. The artist, whoever he was, had undoubtedly been inspired by the propaganda posters of old, with wholesome couples strolling amidst verdant shrubbery, backed by a sky of mythical blue. In reality, however, the only suggestion of nature on this jammed thoroughfare was the line of stark tree trunks, still bare from winter, which grew eight or nine stories from the pavement and served as housing to a raucous mass of crows.

These giant fowl, so endemic to Beijing, had always been likened to a spirit of malevolence in Chinese mythology, as evidenced by the well-known proverb "all crows are equally black," in which crows were equated to officialdom, while black was the color of evil. Although the expression originated back in the Qing dynasty, it was still perceived as relevant in the current era, especially when applied to the Party elite and their acolytes whose corrupt influence affected every aspect of daily life.

It meant that if Zhao's own self-image was that of the dutiful ox, then the permanent ruling regime could easily be visualized as the crows circling above, making their noise and casting their shadows while the beast of burden tries to stand his ground and plow his furrows. Should he ever stumble, they would undoubtedly be upon him in an instant, feeding on the carrion until his carcass was stripped to the bone.

These were the kind of gruesome images his mind sometimes conjured up when he was discouraged and he was almost glad when they were interrupted by something as mundane as the traffic ahead of him starting to move. Traveling like this had been a mistake and

Zhao was beginning to wonder if car ownership, for so long his goal, was as great a symbol of success as he'd always believed.

That was when his cell rang. He was concerned that it might be his client demanding to know how much progress he'd made but it wasn't Anders. It was Zhao's wife, calling long distance. He hadn't spoken to her, or to their fourteen-year-old daughter, in over a week but he was pleased to hear her voice. They'd been living separate lives for a long time, not out of choice but necessity, for the sake of income, which had been an ongoing struggle throughout his life.

Back when he was no older than his current tenants, he taught himself rudimentary language skills from purloined Hollywood videos and passed himself off as a fluent interpreter to recruiting agents who knew no better. When the opportunity finally arose, Zhao grabbed it gratefully, traveling northeast to the industrial town of Changchun. The position was to help German expatriates at a new car plant communicate with their Chinese counterparts, because while most of the foreigners had a basic grasp of English, the locals understood not a word—which was fortunate in regard to Zhao's own capabilities. As the man in the middle of such language dysfunction, his own deficiencies were not obvious and with his affable, accommodating personality, he soon became a favorite on both sides of the cultural divide.

It was at about that stage when he met the young woman who would become his wife. As a native of that city, she too found it cold and depressing but they looked to have a future together when she announced one morning that she'd been to the doctor and her suspicions were confirmed. She had a new life inside of her. It was perhaps the greatest moment that Zhao had ever experienced but the good news was short-lived. The marketing division to which he'd been assigned was transferring its operations to Beijing at about the same time that his wife's mother became sick, so with their respective responsibilities, the couple arranged a temporary split. It wouldn't be long, they promised each other, but somehow their brief period apart was now almost a decade.

In theory, Zhao could have returned to Changchun at any point but there was less work available for him there, so he remained here in his own hometown of Beijing where prospects were better—so good, in fact, that he quit his company job in order to take on more lucrative freelance projects in the hope that this might bring the family back together sooner.

As an entrepreneurial endeavor, it was a bold move with a great deal of potential, yet it also proved to be a less stable source of income, which didn't sit well with his ox-like sense of responsibility and why he ultimately decided to take in young tenants. It meant he now had a well-earned reputation plus a certain degree of security but sadly, wistfully, he was still six hundred miles from the people he loved and no closer to getting them back.

"How's the new car?" his wife was asking him.

He thought about telling her what she wanted to hear, that it was wonderful, that people were very impressed, but he was too honest for that. "Not as much fun as I thought it was going to be," he confessed.

"Maybe you should drive it up here so we can all take a ride in it."

"All the way to Changchun?"

"Why not?"

"Well, for one thing, there's my work here."

"Take a few days off."

"A few days? How can I do that? Work is work. Nobody pays me for vacations."

At that, there was a period of silence on the line because there was no possible answer she could offer. "How's it going in the city?" she asked him eventually. "Are the students still demonstrating?"

"Maybe. Probably. I mean, Liang and Chen were just getting ready as I was leaving this morning. I believe that's where they're going."

"You know what your daughter said yesterday? She said that if she were there, she'd be going out with them to protest the pollution."

"I hope you told her what you thought of that idea."

"She thinks it's glamorous what they're doing."

"Tell her it's not glamorous at all, it's . . . it's crazy."

"Why would I do that? Why start an argument? I just told her she's not there, so it's not possible."

There was another long pause as he tried to imagine what he would say to his daughter if he were up there right now. It made him realize that he'd probably just end up quarreling with her, which contrasted vividly with the tranquil prudence of his wife.

He was still holding the phone when the blur of tears came to his eyes, causing the red taillights ahead of him to dissolve within their own pools of color. For the most part, he'd learned to tolerate the painful loneliness of his existence but these random moments of emotion seemed to be happening more frequently as he entered his middle years and sometimes they were simply beyond his control.

LIANG 梁

Some people were contrarian by nature, their sole task in life being to challenge the status quo, to rail against authority just because it existed, but Liang was not one of them. Her live-in partner, Chen, might have that kind of mentality but she most certainly did not and she'd only agreed to go along with him because she sincerely believed that this state of environmental degradation could not continue.

Beijing was bad but her home province, neighboring Hebei, was far worse. Many communities there had come to be known as "cancer villages" due to the extent of that lethal affliction and the high rate of premature death. The soil was contaminated by chemicals and there were no longer any earthworms to keep it organically productive. Many of the lakes and rivers on which they depended glowed green with algae because effluence was dumped in raw, turning all fish, livestock and crops noxious. And she'd heard it was the same in many other parts of the country. Even the great Yangtze River, where Mao once swam, was almost dead. Would he dare swim there now, she wondered? The nation was rapidly poisoning itself and somebody had to do something.

That's why she was with Chen this morning, waiting on the sidewalk for their lift, but it was hard to converse while they were wearing their filtration masks, so they just stood there, lost in the murk and their own silent worlds, trying to breathe as best they could. Again, she was considering whether to stay with this young man who was so much her opposite. Today was the collective protest, a time to stand together, to remain loyal to each other and to the group but would that still be relevant next week, next month, next year? Did she really want him as the father of her future child or was she really just staying with him because she was alone in the city without a *hukou*? And if so, did that make her no better than a common prostitute? It was a question she'd asked herself many times already, always finding some reason in the daily struggle to cast it aside, to avoid the personal crisis it would instigate.

When they met, it was under the most mundane of circumstances, in a fast-food restaurant of all places, where she'd taken shelter from a winter downpour. The place was packed, as it always seemed to be at lunch hour, with customers obliged to place their plastic trays down on anyone's table without even asking, wherever they could find space to squat. It was noisy, smelly and steamy as coats and hoods dried out but when Chen grinned at her as she squeezed in next to him, it was like a beam of sunshine on a miserable day and they started to chat.

At the time, they were each sharing accommodations with strangers and were both looking for some kind of improvement. After that first meeting, they didn't date as much as share information—about buildings that weren't too filthy or landlords who didn't demand too big a bribe to consider an application. In a way, it was fun sharing the experience of apartment hunting, so when they at last found a room with Zhao, a man of rare integrity who asked for nothing beyond good character and an assured rent, it seemed natural for Chen to suggest they take advantage of this good fortune together.

It would be a platonic agreement, he took pains to assure her, but of course, she'd been initially worried that he wouldn't keep his word. Yet as it turned out, he wasn't pushy at all and they spent the first few weeks wrapped tightly in their own blankets. But having been thrown together in such a tight area, almost tripping over each other unclothed in the night, the eventual outcome was both obvious and understandable—or so she rationalized. And while she didn't enjoy the sex as much as he did, she was in some way comforted by the presence of another human who treated her with a modicum of dignity. It wasn't an ideal arrangement but it was tolerable and it allowed her to put off, at least for a while, any thoughts that were more existential.

Now she found herself with him on the street, sharing not just his bed but also his ideals, a paradoxical arrangement because, in truth, she didn't even wish to consider bringing a child into this contaminated world.

ANDERS

An experienced globetrotter, Anders knew that etiquette demanded he consume a certain amount of local food, that it was discourteous, even offensive to certain hosts if he didn't appear to appreciate it. When he was on his own, however, his preference was to eat whatever he felt like eating at that moment in time, especially at breakfast, whether that happened to be a bowl of grain cereal with yogurt when he was in health mode, or like this morning, a grease-laden platter of eggs and bacon delivered promptly by room service with toast, jam and a tall pot of coffee.

In between mouthfuls, he continued sending and receiving the cryptic and often caustic emails for which he was legendary, pausing only briefly to scan headlines or alerts as soon as they arrived.

One notification that caught his attention was from the local US Embassy website, which gave him a realistic measure of the Beijing air quality. Unlike official government readings, which even now tended to be overly optimistic, the figures from the monitoring equipment on the roof of the eight-floor building were a far more honest assessment of the conditions—so much so that local residents had taken to spreading word from this unauthorized source as if they were passing on classified material.

The correct particle count at any given hour, as well as the on-going number of "blue sky" days, had become a must-know obsession, as much as the market listings or the basketball scores. The fact that the Americans even published this information annoyed the ministerial authorities immensely but since the embassy was sovereign territory, there was little they could do to shut down the site without diplomatic repercussions. What had begun as a minor service for employees and expatriates had grown into something of a cause célèbre throughout the larger community.

Once Anders had finished eating, he took a cool shower and dressed in his most conservative style. The only difference between his own clothes and those of the other attendees of the National Congress was that his suit had been custom-made on London's Savile Row and instead of a red flag in his lapel, his preferred pin would be the emblems of both nations, the five stars of China crossed with the fifty of the US, a visible gesture of bilateral friendship.

Within half an hour, he was ready. All he needed now was for his three colleagues to show up: his vice president, Tse; his joint venture partner, Huang; and of course, his redoubtable interpreter, Zhao, without whom Anders wouldn't be able to understand a word of the proceedings.

While he'd mastered a few podium-worthy phrases of Chinese to be polite to an audience, he'd never bothered with any more because it hadn't been necessary. Everywhere he landed, no matter which continent, the people he met either spoke or were desperately trying to learn English, so why bother cluttering his own head with *their* grammar and syntax? He had enough problems to worry him and anyway, as with cuisine, the art of speaking a foreign language was no cultural pleasure for him, just an inconvenience, an interruption to the business of doing business, and he preferred to avoid it.

3

That day, we were not forewarned.

CHEN 陈

Until their lift arrived, Chen had been tense, brooding, but as soon as the sedan pulled up, his personality changed, a complete metamorphosis, a rapid shift from disquiet to exuberance. He held the door for Liang and they slid into the back. Up front, it was their friend Sun who was driving, even though the elegant vehicle belonged to his girlfriend, Feng, in the passenger seat.

"What's the word?" Chen said immediately to Sun. "Are we still on? How many do you think will show? Any more news about security?"

Sun, an angular figure, leaned his head over with that lopsided charm of his. "Which question do you want me to answer?"

If anyone could claim to be one of the de facto leaders of these public manifestations, it was Sun, whose real talent was in growing and maintaining his *guanxi*, that most critical of all group dynamics. In contemporary China, this meant more than networking, even more than friendship, because in a ruthless system with no equitable recourse for suffering or abuse, the only defense came from being surrounded by a circle of trust—and that was the purpose, the very essence, of *guanxi*. It wasn't a club or union, nor was it a construct of social media. It was simply a tight agglomeration of advice, assistance and favors that were given and received freely whether for promotion or protection, allowing a figure like Sun to define exactly where to place his confidence and on whom he could rely.

It was also why his information was usually so accurate and why Chen was now pumping him to find out more. He needed to know the scope of things, not just for the sake of Liang but for his own professional requirements as an investigative blogger.

"All right, fine," said Sun, just to calm his passenger down. "Here's what we know as of this morning. Nothing at all."

"Excuse me?"

"You want guarantees on numbers? I don't have any."

"I don't want guarantees, I want intelligence."

"You know as much as I do."

Chen waited, just to find out if there was any more forthcoming. "We can't just show up blind," he said. "That's stupid."

"We're not blind. We just have less than optimal . . . visibility."

Sun grinned at his own clever twist on the weather but it failed to impress his friend.

"I'm serious," Chen insisted.

"You want to skip today?"

"No, I don't want to skip today. I just want to know what we're letting ourselves in for."

"I told you, I don't know."

Chen was becoming impatient. "You must know something. We've been out two days already."

Sun sighed. "What do you want me to tell you? Who knows what decisions have been made behind closed doors? You think the militia sends me their plans by email? You think I have a password into their computer system?"

Chen sat back in frustration, mainly because he knew that the objections were valid. There was just no information about security intentions from any source. True, there had been speeches by several ministers about the need to repair the environmental damage, including a member of the Politburo who had called for the public to voice their support on the topic. In fact, it was this vague utterance which had become the generally accepted approval allowing them to demonstrate at Tiananmen. But as Sun was implying, nobody in the leadership had followed through on that initial permission and no authority had given its definitive assent: neither the police, the militia, the army, nor any other branch of state security. The dangers of proceeding were therefore evident.

WEI 魏

Seizing a rare quiet moment, the veteran Corporal Wei leaned against the armored transport and drew on his cigarette. He knew the habit might kill him but didn't care too much, because he'd heard that these days even the polluted air could poison his lungs.

It was how things were and he felt he had no right to any opinion. It wasn't his place. He was an ordinary soldier in the militia, just like his father before him, and it happened to be a life he preferred. His basic needs were met, he had many friends and as long as he didn't talk too much about things that didn't concern him, he had few worries and even fewer regrets.

Wei had been just a young recruit, new to Beijing from his home province of Yunnan, when Deng ordered the capital detachments of both the regular army and Wei's own militia to march on Tiananmen. At the time, he'd understood the necessity, not that he'd ever been asked, and it all appeared to be clear enough. As they explained at the time, the state could not allow social harmony to be disrupted by the unsanctioned element they called *baotu*, troublemakers, some of whom were protesting too strenuously.

It could lead to anarchy, even to counterrevolution, and that could not be tolerated. The message had to be sent to the people in the square and shock therapy was the only way. That's what they'd said and Wei had listened. He didn't especially enjoy killing—he found it to be a messy, unpredictable business—but he wasn't ignorant to the fact that wearing the militia uniform made it an occasional duty.

He was remembering at this moment because earlier in the morning, he'd been taken aside by Chief Sergeant Guan for a private discussion. The regiment knew that Wei was the only man left who'd been involved back then and Guan was asking him questions about morale, about remorse, to which Wei just shrugged. He found it hard to respond because, to him, these issues were irrelevant. When they were ordered to fire, they fired. If, instead, they'd been ordered to give the students tea and moon cakes, they'd have done that, too.

Then came the sergeant's final query. If required to do it again today, would he follow that order? Would his unit? But the only answer Wei could give was to nod. Of course he would. If that was the order, what choice did he have? What choice did the platoon have? Either obey or face a court-martial and when found guilty—a verdict always decided in advance—they would no doubt face a firing squad. And when the sergeant probed further, testing the limits, asking the corporal if he thought that was unfair or unjust, Wei again had no answer, because that's just how it was. That's how it had been for his father and how it would always be.

SUN 孙

Each new day of protest was additional cause for concern and Sun, as one of the organizers, couldn't allow himself to falsify the possibilities. He preferred that people were aware of the realities, because unlike most of his contemporaries, he knew what prison was all about. He'd been to visit his older brother many times over the years in a penitentiary on the outskirts of Shanghai.

Back at the start of their respective careers, the best advice from many quarters was to find a job in government. Employment by a particular division or department wasn't as important as being secure within Party ranks, becoming one of the administrative elite, and who knows, perhaps even having a chance at some point in the future to rise above the melee and become a crow. Nobody liked crows, it was well-known, but that didn't mean it wasn't immensely beneficial to have such a protective element within the family.

And so, Sun's brother took his parents' counsel and managed, through his own diligence, to gain a trainee position within the Ministry of Public Works, where he labored hard and generally tried to stay out of trouble. His only problem was that he was far too principled for his own good.

All ministries and just about all corporations, whether state or private, were rife with corrupt practices, most of them so ingrained into the organizational culture that it was difficult to imagine conducting affairs, negotiating contracts, or maintaining relationships in any other way. Unfortunately, Sun's brother recognized this too late. As he progressed, he was included in more files, more arrangements, and began to notice discrepancies, some carefully masked but others totally blatant.

When he asked about them, he was told by colleagues to mind his place but then made a fatal error by taking his observations to his supervisor, which marked him not as a conscientious employee but as a potential malcontent. Yet even then, nothing happened until investigations were triggered by a senior Party connection who felt he wasn't receiving his fair allowance and in retribution used his influence with the inquisitors of Finance. That led to panic within certain echelons of Public Works.They knew that nothing would go away unless there was somebody to accuse, some sacrificial goat who could be blamed whether there was evidence or not. The obvious answer was the one who'd been bleating, the only virtuous individual in the department, Sun's brother, who was duly prosecuted and imprisoned when his only fault was naiveté.

Since that time, Sun had been visiting his sibling in the cell block whenever he had the chance. He'd seen the conditions, the misery and the filth, and had spent many years talking and writing, as diplomatically as possible, in order to get his brother's sentence reviewed but all to no avail. He even hired a law firm, spending a great deal of his salary as a junior architect in addition to an inordinate amount of time, but discovered like so many before him that the concept of justice in the one-party system was almost nonexistent. Despite all the funds expended, nothing happened. The poor bleating goat remained behind those thick walls in Shanghai, an enemy of the crows, with little hope of escape.

The situation caused their parents endless grief but there was nothing more Sun could do. The only positive result of any of it was that he'd met Feng, who'd recently graduated and had just started her employment in the Beijing office of the law firm he'd hired. When Sun exhausted his resources, she continued helping him pro bono because she admired his efforts and that's when the attraction became mutual.

FENG 封

Of the group of four in the car that morning, only Feng came from a family of means and, indeed, it was her automobile that Sun was now driving on their way to the protest.

Having money to spend didn't embarrass Feng, despite the fact that this was a more expensive model than their modest passengers, Liang and Chen, could ever dream of affording. Today, millionaires were commonplace and even billionaires were not that unusual, so living in a suburb like Shunyi and purchasing only the most premium western brands was a fairly standard, even clichéd, way of life. Wealth had become mainstream in this modern version of China and over a third of the country, a population the size of the entire European Union, counted themselves among the middle class. As for the rest—the laborers, the farm workers, the students, the migrants, the unemployed—it was widely accepted that they would have to catch up as best they could. In this new era, the societal currency was either affluence or influence and the only people who cared about anything else were the few like Feng who bothered to have a conscience.

For this morality, she credited her mother, a primary school teacher, far more than her father, a distinguished cardiologist within the privileged cocoon of private healthcare. It was why Feng had initially helped Sun, even before she knew him very well, and why she'd assisted so many similar clients under the non-authorized *weiquan* legal program of reduced fees for worthy cases, a system of rectitude still largely absent within the judicial structure.

It was also why she was here on this day. Like her boyfriend, Feng was well aware that each person in the vehicle, and no doubt each of those they were about to meet, had his or her own reasons for the protest that was about to take place. For herself, of course, the main issue was the misapplication of juristic principle and the act of holding it hostage to the Party's interests. For Sun, it was his ongoing obsession with the appalling fate of his brother. For their friend, Liang, it was the lack of all welfare rights in the city for the simple want of a *hukou*.

And for Chen, the journalist, it was not only the smothering censorship but also the deliberate spew of disinformation, a nationwide plague that had become acceptable under the rationale of social peace. Ostensibly, they were all banding together because of the polluted environment but that was just a noble excuse, a rallying cause with which everyone could identify. The underlying truth was that each of them had deep personal grievances against the regime that now ran this ancient land, a profound resentment on so many levels that the pressurized anger was barely contained.

GUAN 關

Unlike his corporal, Chief Sergeant Class 2 Guan had the aptitude to advance in the modern military, with new technologies to learn, strategies to master, new ways of managing men and machines that were more appropriate to the nation's emergence as a major power.

Yet some things had never changed and Guan was aware that even now, every battalion of the army, every sector of police, every division of his own service, the PLA militia, had its cadre of political officers, each of whom reported directly back to the Party. He wasn't sure of the exact loyalties involved but he knew who the people were in his own regiment. He even exchanged the occasional greeting with them, although he made sure to be careful with the words he used.

What he didn't know, however, was how many others there might be, how many had been placed secretly in position with the task of spying on their own comrades. It was those people and not the more obvious political officers for whom Sergeant Guan and his platoon had to be on constant guard. A simple slip, a few words of complaint, a joke in poor taste—it could all be noted down and reported. There was even a story going around one time about a private who was arrested after talking in his sleep. Guan wasn't sure he believed that but it served as a warning all the same.

In many ways, it reminded him of the small town where he grew up back in Shaanxi, where there'd once been an old woman on his street who betrayed all the daily gossip in the same way. She was so infirm, she could hardly move from her own doorstep but she seemed to watch and hear everything that was going on, day or night. She knew who was out late, who drank, who got pregnant and which kids stole things. Guan's parents had loathed that old woman, as did everyone in the neighborhood, but they also said it was good training for the larger world and when Guan joined the army, it was his father who warned him of such people. They will watch you and report you, Guan was warned, so don't tell anyone what you're doing, where you're going, or who gave you the orders and make sure those around you know that, otherwise they can get you into trouble.

The advice was especially important on a day like this, he felt, when the duty officer informed him that they would be heading for sensitive duty at Tiananmen and, once again, he wondered who around him might be an informant. He had his suspicions, of course, but he had no way of knowing for sure, nor were any of them completely certain about *him*. He'd never been approached to do anything of the kind and that alone made him wonder why not. Did the authorities have their doubts about him? The notion had crossed his mind on more than one occasion.

Once his detail was packed and settled into the five transport buses, Guan climbed aboard each in turn, instructing every platoon not to be provoked into any rash behavior, no matter what the circumstances, because these were the orders that had been handed down. He also told them that since they would be out in public, right in the center of the city, their actions were being monitored far more closely than usual, so they were to be careful, very careful, with every action they undertook. Unless otherwise commanded, they were to remain passive.

"Do you know what passive means, Corporal Wei?" Guan asked the veteran, who was in charge of one of the buses.

"Yes, Chief Sergeant."

"What does it mean? Please tell us."

"It means we do nothing unless told, Chief Sergeant."

"Correct, Corporal Wei. So make sure you don't and that means all of you. I'll be watching. *Others* will be watching."

Guan glanced around at all of them, his expression ominous, then without saying another word, he left to repeat the performance on the next bus and each one after that. Only once he was done did the drivers start the engines and pull out, the intention being to travel in convoy with a police escort all the way from the southwestern barracks into the heart of the capital.

SUN 孙

Instead of taking the direct route into the city, Sun drove Feng's elegant sedan the long way around via the 3rd Ring Road, making surprisingly good time to the Chaoyang district, just east of central.

By now, daylight had more or less arrived, such as it was, but the sand still coated many surfaces and the smog was so thick they could hardly see across the main Jianguo Road.

With a little more visibility, they might have been able to make out the famous new headquarters of Central China Television, known even in Chinese by its English abbreviation CCTV, an extraordinary architectural project in which the senior partners of Sun's firm had participated. It was only on a sub-contractual basis but nevertheless, it was a major accomplishment just to be able to say they were involved, even if the building had become controversial. A counter-intuitive rhomboid shape, it had already been labeled "Big Boxer Shorts" by a cynical public and was therefore in competition with structures like the "Bird's Nest" and the "Water Cube," as well as the "Donut" and even the "Phallus," to be the most outrageous of the modernistic creations, all financed by easy money and brought to fruition by egotistical visions from every continent.

Multiplying the scorn for the CCTV building, however, was the comedy of errors in which workers celebrated its completion by setting off illegal fireworks from the roof, thereby causing a fountain of sparks, which in turn burned down the giant luxury hotel that was still under construction right next door. To the government, the incident became a humiliation, while to the public, this proud symbol of the new China had simply turned into a whispered joke. As for Sun's firm, they just shrugged and went on with business because there was little else they could do. This was Beijing and just like the weather, such things tended to happen here.

The travel plan was to park in his own reserved spot under the company's offices at the Wanda Plaza complex, then take the subway at nearby Dawanglu over to Tiananmen. The only problem would be if they accidentally ran into any of his colleagues in the vicinity, because he'd already called in sick today but, luckily, that didn't happen.

They did, however, cross paths with a member of the janitorial staff who was out supervising a contingent of eight cleaning ladies, mops in hand and masks over their faces, washing the exterior flagstones. Sun glanced at them with an expression of sympathy but none looked up or dared to respond in any way. Any critical word from a superior would be grounds for dismissal and there were always a thousand rural migrants just waiting in line for the job.

Sometimes these menial workers didn't get paid at all. When Sun was hired, this entire area was still under construction—a major excavation project just to rebuild the drainage—and he was saddened to see that the laborers were living for months in squalid tents right on the muddy site, freezing in the cold and sweltering in the heat without even knowing whether there would be a few yuan at the end of it. Apparently, the foreman had told them that all wages would depend on the boss and his cash flow but since none of the workers had any clue what a cash flow might be, all they could do was continue and trust that at the end of it all, they'd have at least something to send to their impoverished families back in their home provinces.

Like Liang, they had no *hukou* but unlike her, they had nothing at all: no resident friends, no dry apartment, no prospects at all. They just drifted into the capital on hope and stayed on the adrenaline of their fear. And every day, Sun was required to walk past these sad souls to enter his pristine office, where he received the kind of salary that, although not lavish, certainly allowed a talented young man to enjoy his pleasant lifestyle, meeting friends after work at the jazz club and dating professional career women like Feng.

In fact, he shouldn't even be here, he told himself, when he still had so many projects to complete up in that same office. It made him wonder, not for the first time, why he was even helping to organize these demonstrations. True, his brother was still rotting in that hellhole of a jail but how would protesting the climate help his cause? Would it obtain a release? Highlight the injustice? Do anything at all?

As Feng often said, it was the duty of the young to improve society and in principle he agreed with her but was that a good enough reason to risk everything, or was it simply too vague to accomplish anything? That was the uncertainty as he struggled across the complex with his friends, trying not to inhale the nauseous fumes or swallow the microscopic grit that seemed to swirl in the vortex of the buildings.

LIANG 梁

Due to her lack of stable income as well as her mild personality, Liang knew that her main vulnerability was self-confidence. While she fully believed in today's moral crusade and had just as much reason to protest due to the advanced state of pollution in her own home province, the real reason she came along was because she was a relief bank teller and had little else to do.

She didn't love Chen who was right next to her, arm around her shoulders, nor could she really relate to Sun or Feng, who were nice enough but whose lifestyle she could hardly imagine. They seemed to have it so easy when it was difficult for her even to foresee the day when she wouldn't have to worry about how to afford the most basic necessities and how she could possibly spare anything to send back to her family. Yet despite all of that, here she was, sharing the social conscience of these people she hardly knew and facing the perils of official punishment should the worst scenario occur.

The subway station, when they finally reached it, was filled to capacity as usual and as they maneuvered their way toward the westbound platform, she could feel Chen holding her hand tightly. It was his way of protecting her, of showing her he cared, and she wasn't sure whether she should be accepting his devotion so readily. She felt it was not just unfair on her part, it was hypocritical, but she let it happen it anyway.

She allowed him to love her, to *make* love to her, and that made her . . . She still couldn't bear to admit it even to herself. But more and more, she'd come to realize that she was just playing semantics and knew all too well that soon she'd have to come to terms with it. Could she stay with this young man merely for the sake of that accursed *hukou*? And even more depraved, would she find it an easier decision if he had more money, if they shared the living standards of Sun and Feng?

For reasons that perhaps had more to do with her own small-town morality than with her big-city relationship, these questions both bothered and perplexed her.

CHEN 陈

They stood tightly together on the train, hemmed in on all sides by crosstown commuters, many still wearing their outside masks:

bleary-eyed office staff carrying breakfast into work, fussy mothers with fold-up strollers taking their toddlers to kindergarten, self-absorbed students with their shoulder bags and cell phones, stoic seniors bemused by everything around them. And in all the crush, Chen tried to hold on to Liang as closely as possible. There were just too many perverts down here who used these rides as an opportunity to touch, rub, or even expose.

But beyond the suspicion, he gazed at all the faces around him with journalistic interest. Who were these people? Where did they come from and what were their stories? Like so many in his profession, he fought a constant internal battle about whether to expound on major themes like state policy and global shifts, or to focus in on personal details, all the tiny, telling moments that revealed a larger perspective. Indeed, that was exactly how it was when he ran a story about Liang, a journalistic probe into the inequities of the *hukou* system. He could have approached the story from either angle and that was his personal dichotomy.

It wasn't so much that he hadn't yet found a salaried position but that he hadn't yet formed a clear profile of himself, of exactly what kind of reporter he wanted to be, and he kept wishing that his destiny in this regard would somehow show itself as if by spiritual revelation. While the government, in its own search for philosophy, had recently taken to reinstating the work of Confucius, as if an ancient sage had any relevance in this modern world, Chen was far more prosaic in his beliefs. He preferred to think that his salvation would come from perseverance, from rigorous objectivity, from meticulous standards, from his own earnest quest for the truth.

And so he wrote his blog, maintained his *guanxi*, practiced his English and hoped that someday one of his carefully crafted pieces would capture enough attention to go viral, bringing him his long-sought share of readership and respect. In his mind, this was the only reason he was even taking this wild chance with his longtime friend, Sun, who he first met at college. He was thinking that being so close to one of the organizers of this extraordinary event might be the opportunity for which he'd been waiting.

The fact that he was bringing Liang along with him—Liang, who was so close to him now that he could feel her warmth—was just an extra bonus, a coincidental addition that might help keep them together through what he assumed was a mutual interest. In his own way, he cared for her deeply and could easily imagine himself spending his life with her, having a child with her, but only once he'd established himself on a more permanent basis. Living in Zhao's spare room was no life for anyone, much less a married couple, and he longed for the career breakthrough that would act as a passport to all his ambitions.

Perhaps today, he thought. Perhaps today. It was a phrase that had turned into his own mental refrain.

4 *That day, many were delayed.*

ZHAO 赵

While his tenants had already reached the city core, Zhao was still in his car, still checking the time and still fretting that he should have planned his route better, asked for advice, or even weighed the logical benefits of car versus subway.

While his fanciful idea had been to show off his new acquisition, in reality he'd be parking in the hotel's underground garage long before his client would have the possibility of admiring it. In effect, it meant that the only reason he'd made this decision was so he'd be able to mention that he'd driven here in his brand-new vehicle. It was ludicrous, thought Zhao, to generate this level of vanity. Not only that, it was self-defeating, because a busy man like Anders would be so upset at the tardiness that there'd be no conversational space at all during which to talk about anything.

He was on Fuxing Lu and approaching the 2nd Ring Road underpass when the congestion became solid, with nothing moving at all. But at least here he could actually observe the reason for the holdup. Approaching from the south was some kind of long column, perhaps military, escorted by several police cruisers, their flashing blue lights piercing the thick haze like ghostly apparitions. They had the authority to do more or less as they pleased, from closing off streets to arresting anyone who complained, so when they appeared in the city en masse like this, few dared to object.

Even taxi drivers, normally the most contrary of individuals, chose to wait in their own disgruntled silence. They'd been ordered to exchange their squat, smelly cabs for larger, cleaner vehicles but that only made matters worse due to increased leasing charges, which in turn led to increased fares, resulting in an overall decrease in their revenues. Zhao was parked between two of them now and he could almost sense their indignation at this latest affront. This was more than just the usual traffic congestion. This time they were being held up deliberately by some idiot army maneuver.

Like them, Zhao had already guessed that this unusual show of force had to do with the ongoing protests, especially as they related to this first day of the Party Congress, and it made him a little uneasy knowing that the two young people who rented his room might be involved.

Once again, it was confirmation of his unshakable belief that people should learn from history and not be obliged to relive it.

TSE 谢

As the aircraft continued to circle above the dense atmosphere, Tse was thinking about her years in Vancouver, about the mountains and the ocean and the clarity of the heavens. All too often, she recalled, there'd be a rain mist which would obscure those idyllic views but it was nothing like the smog of Beijing. It was clean—it even tasted clean—and sometimes she'd go for a walk on the damp beach, stepping across the driftwood as she gazed out across the whitecaps toward her alma mater, UBC, on the opposite peninsula.

It was in that city she first met Anders. He'd just become head of the North American division and was already on the inside track to global management. She remembered that the staff laid on a nice after-five affair to welcome him, nothing too sumptuous, just a locally produced wine, a few plates of canapés and some polite chit-chat. She'd made a good presentation that afternoon, speaking well and answering all of his questions, so when he eased his way over to speak to her, she thought it would be to follow up on a few points—but that's not what came out of his mouth.

"I presume you speak *putonghua?*" he said.

The fact that he even knew the word surprised her and for the moment she was uncharacteristically flustered. Normally, she was the most assured of people.

"As a matter of fact, I don't," she replied. "Not very well."

"You're from Hong Kong, I understand? Originally, I mean."

"Yes, well, that's to say I was born in Kowloon but my family only spoke Cantonese."

"So I guess you'll have to start brushing up."

"I will?"

"I would think so."

"With respect, there's not really a lot of *putonghua* spoken in Vancouver."

"I'm aware of that," he replied, as if it were common knowledge. "But I'm looking down the road and I suggest you might wish to do the same."

Then he did a strange thing. He offered her his glass to clink, as if in a toast, as if they were locking in some confidential agreement to which she wasn't yet privy.

What she did notice, however, was the bronzed left hand that held the glass had a distinct white bar across the fourth finger. It was as if he'd been wearing a ring for a long time but had recently removed it. Of course, she said nothing but it did make her a little wary about whether this cryptic interchange was just a surreptitious way of intracompany flirting and if so, all she could think about was the kind of excuse she could offer. She couldn't decide if his approach was flattering or creepy but either way, her refusal would be adamant because she'd begun to realize, even back within the dorms of her university, that she enjoyed the company of other females—as much and sometimes even more than males—both for friendship and for intimacy.

She was therefore relieved on this occasion when there was no follow-up, none at all. He went on his way the next morning and she didn't communicate with him directly for several years, not until she was in the UK at the large office on Canary Wharf with her career progressing nicely. By that stage, he'd reached the pinnacle, the global equivalent of the corner office, and it was not long after this anointment by the board that the unexpected phone call came through from New York. There was little small talk and his voice was all business.

"How would you feel about moving back to Hong Kong?"

"From here? Have I done something wrong?"

At the time, there was an expression in England known as "FILTH," an acronym for the phrase "Failed In London, Try Hong Kong." For locals, it was nothing more than a teasing derogatory, a center-of-the-empire cliché targeted at those who would leave, yet for someone like Tse, it was hurtful—and besides, she'd spent most of her life advancing the other way.

"It's not a backward step," he said, "I can assure you."

"It's not?"

"How about if I told you we'll rent you a place on the Peak?"

As the name suggested, this was the highest point on the island, populated with people who owned half-million-dollar limousines and who smashed hundred-year-old bottles of cognac just because they could.

"Excuse me?"

"As vice president for East Asia, you'll need a decent place to call home, won't you?"

Ever since she entered the company, she'd been ambitious, always gunning for one promotion or another, but she was genuinely stunned by this development. "I don't know what to say."

"Lot to take in, right? Listen, gotta run. I'll be flying over to Europe next week. Let's do lunch, okay?"

"Yes . . . yes, fine, of course. I'll look forward to it."

"Great, I'll be in touch."

And that's how it began: first the offer, then the move and then the brief affair, one after the other in heady succession.

As it happened, the physical aspect of their relationship began at a conference in Maui, when he invited her to stay on afterward for some rest and relaxation. Far more mature than before, she sensed what he had in mind but chose to accept the offer anyway as a personal experiment. It had been a long while since she'd been with a man, any man, but it turned out to be a fun week. He was cool and considerate, not at all the alpha behavior she might have feared, and they laughed a lot. In its own way, it was actually a wonderful episode, a romantic fantasy come to life, but it couldn't last because she couldn't change who she was. Then, over dinner on that final evening, he did indeed ask if she'd like to continue the relationship in some way but she declined with as much charm as she could muster, using the easy excuse of geographic distance and the sheer difficulty for a pair of globetrotters to maintain any kind of meaningful contact.

Thankfully, he seemed to accept her explanation with good grace and that was the end of it, with no apparent harm done to her career trajectory. Yet she often wondered if he suspected her lie. He was, after all, fairly astute. But after much hindsight reflection, she felt she'd handled the dilemma extremely well, offering herself a generous measure of kudos for both her poise and composure.

She hadn't thought about all this in some time but being stuck in a metal tube circling pointlessly above the smog seemed to have its own way of focusing the brain on strange things—and she was only interrupted from this unusual bout of nostalgia by the captain's voice once again. This time he was informing them that, regretfully, the smog was not lifting and that due to fuel supplies, he had no choice but to land at Tianjin. There were audible groans from around the aircraft. The distance from that large coastal city back to the capital was almost a hundred miles on one of the most congested highways in the country, so it was of no consolation at all when she and her fellow passengers were asked to accept the airline's apologies before being informed that a fleet of buses was being organized for their convenience.

Obviously, theirs wouldn't be the only flight being diverted and Tse knew that both the airport and all nearby hotels would be in turmoil. She also knew that a road journey like that could take most of the day if not more, ever since she'd heard about the quagmire not long ago when all vehicles along that particular highway came to an absolute standstill for an entire three days, nothing moving in that time at all.

For Tse, the net result was that she would have to forget today's special agenda and prepare herself instead for an extended period of misery and frustration.

ANDERS

He was in the restaurant, glancing absently through a hotel copy of *China Daily* while waiting for Tse and Huang. He was still secretly hoping that neither of them would show up to disturb his tranquility when in walked his interpreter, a little red-faced from the shame of being late.

"I'm so sorry," said Zhao as he over-pumped his client's hand.

"Relax, you're not that late. Sit down, have a coffee."

"It was traffic, just terrible on a day like this."

"It's okay, no problem."

"Plus, the army was out . . ."

"The army?"

"Well, it might have been the militia, I don't know. All this security, with the protests and everything. I'm sure it's all, you know, necessary, but it doesn't help the traffic situation."

Anders understood that this was as far as a man like Zhao would ever dare go in his criticism of authority and he felt duty-bound to respect the same parameters.

"The weather doesn't help," he replied.

Here, too, the idea of "weather" was a safe euphemism for man-made problems like city pollution mixed with desert deforestation. With a word like that, there was no undue condemnation implied, which was the accepted way of speaking in China. Despite all the trophy buildings and western-style consumerism, this was still an authoritarian state and nobody was ever completely sure who might be listening or what mental notes they might be taking. It might be somebody here in the hotel, even the waiter who was now pouring coffee, which was why Zhao instinctively stopped speaking and only resumed once the man was out of earshot.

"And how are you these days?" he said to Anders, adding extra cream and sugar to his beverage.

"I'm well, thanks, couldn't be better. And yourself?"

"Also fine, thank you."

Despite the longstanding relationship, their discussions were often on this kind of formal basis, a practice that Zhao always seemed to assume was more professional but which Anders believed was a direct result of the necessary caution. There was a pause while he thought of something else to ask.

"How's the family? Still up there in . . . Changchun, is it?"

"Yes, thank you for remembering. They're fine, too."

"Must be tough, being so far away all the time. Ever get up to visit?"

"I try but it's difficult. We do chat online though, every week if we can."

"All this technology we've got today," said Anders, as if marveling at the miracle of it all. "Hard to imagine how we ever managed without it."

"I agree. Even my new car is equipped with Bluetooth."

Anders hadn't really been paying much attention to this somewhat forced small-talk but fortunately he picked up on that particular comment. "A new car? Hey, congratulations!" he said with an abundance of enthusiasm, before reaching across to shake Zhao's hand.

"Thank you, you're very kind."

There was another lapse in the conversation until they heard a buzz from the cell on the table. Anders picked it up and slid it open, only to hear a slew of Chinese with the name Huang at the end. It was his host for the day and he passed the phone over to his interpreter.

Zhao listened, answered politely and then hung up before returning the device. "Mr. Huang says he's stuck, nothing's moving. He estimates another half-hour at least."

"Too bad. We'll miss the opening."

"He also asked me to say that we're actually not missing anything at all. He says . . ." Zhao hesitated for a moment, glancing around before continuing in a much lower voice. "He says that one speech at the Congress is as boring as the next."

Anders grinned. The comment sounded exactly like Huang, a gregarious rogue with so many high-ranking friends within his aura of influence that he could actually make jokes like that without even considering the fact that he was on an open network.

HUANG 黃

The heavyset man now fuming in the passenger seat of his own Italian supercar was dressed in a pale blue tracksuit, taken directly from his sportswear company's inventory.

For Huang, a native of the southern province of Fujian, this was his usual mode of dress even when conducting business in the national capital. According to legend, he once attended the CCTV auction for the upcoming year's television time in that same outfit and to everyone's astonishment, including many of the corporate elite, he outbid all present to purchase prime broadcast properties worth over a hundred million. He was a *tuhao*, one of the nouveau riche, and he didn't care who knew it.

Normally, he traveled with a full complement of executive advisors from finance, operations, sales and so forth but the only member of staff he had with him today was his driver and bodyguard, because he'd been personally invited to attend the opening session of Congress by the director of sports administration himself. But first he had to go meet his American associate and at the current rate of progress, that might not be for a while, hence the impatience.

Huang had been staying at the Yiheyuan Golf Club, up beyond Kunming Lake in Haidan, where he maintained a suite for these extended visits to the city. In any other global metropolis, a man of his standing would have been zipped across town in his own helicopter but such machines were not allowed in private hands, so he had to make do with mere ground transportation.

He was, however, in the process of having a two-hundred-foot yacht built in France and helping design it was like a hobby to him, a stress-relieving counterpoint to running his business, and he often drove the Cherbourg shipyard to apoplexy with his endless design changes.

The company and the entire source of his wealth was based in the city of Jinjiang, well-known as a global manufacturing center of sporting shoes, clothes and equipment. Here, many of the leading brands had their products developed but Huang had something more, something the others didn't have.

In addition to a large design and production facility, he'd also built the largest sales distribution network in the nation, comprising over five thousand retail stores, all in prime city locations. It was a unique and unrepeatable strategy, planned as if it were a military campaign, with push-pins on highly detailed street maps.

When his real estate representatives found the ideal locale in the most avant-garde neighborhood, he would throw in vast amounts of money to buy out competitors and their properties until he dominated the area. In this manner, he could begin a price war until all in that vicinity had surrendered. Then he would simply shut down all the extraneous stores except one, the most perfectly positioned, and be in total control of his target territory, free to focus on local fashion in terms of design, shape, color, or whatever else his customers desired. After that, he would simply move on to the next city and do exactly the same. It was an irresistible method of expansion, as meticulous as it was inspired, and he'd become extremely prosperous in the process, his net worth close to a billion according to estimates in the financial press.

The most astounding aspect of all this, at least for those who knew him, was that this wasn't even his company. Technically, it belonged to his wife, who had, years before, inherited a small rundown facility on the edge of town from her geriatric father. As was often the habit in traditional households, the young woman was encouraged to marry a man whose most favorable feature was that he could take over the business—and in her case, that man happened to be local boy Huang. He came from a family with good entrepreneurial genes, so he therefore became the chosen one, the savior of the business.

At the start, nobody knew for sure whether this large and noisy youth would succeed but he had a shrewd brain and possessed genuine cunning. As it turned out, he relished the opportunity presented to him and despite his lack of business training—or more likely *because* of it—he generated his own way of doing things, at the start by simple trial and error, before eventually settling on the system he invented.

Along the way, he used his gregarious nature to augment his capitalist instincts by warming up to local party chiefs in each area, without whom nothing could be accomplished, and strove to maintain these hard-won contacts with a regular schedule of monthly bribes and annual gifts despite an ever-growing radius of operation.

To some of the more hypocritical politicians, this was exactly the kind of corruption they claimed they were trying to root out but to Huang, it was simply an investment in his own success, as much a cost of doing business as the raw materials he purchased or the labor force he employed.

One of his special associates in this regard was the director of sports administration, who, for his own substantial recompense, had managed to persuade the CBL, the Chinese Basketball League, to accept Huang's brand as official sponsor.

Since this was by far the most popular sport in the country, easily overshadowing older favorites like badminton and ping-pong, it meant that Huang had, in one stroke, managed to out-maneuver all his domestic competition. While the American NBA was more glamorous even in China, their famous stars were also a hundred times more expensive and he really didn't see the need to compete at that kind of level when his primary strategy was real estate. As long as he kept investing in the best locations, he knew his business would continue its exponential growth.

He even had a notion to take his attack plan abroad, perhaps to Central Africa or the Middle East. Yet in truth, he didn't have full confidence that his methods would actually work there and was afraid that he could waste a great deal of his formidable cash hoard trying to influence the people who ran things in those areas without really knowing what he was doing—which was why he liked to befriend experienced foreign operators like Anders, inviting him along to prestigious events like the National People's Congress while hoping that a little of his worldliness might somehow rub off.

ANDERS

"Just as well he's late," said Anders, speaking of Huang, "because my Hong Kong colleague's not here, either."

"That would be Ms. Tse?" said Zhao.

"It would indeed."

"She's flying this morning?"

"Yeah, I'm guessing the flights are also delayed. You hungry by the way? Feel like some breakfast while you're waiting?"

Zhao appeared tempted but was hesitant about the etiquette. "Are you sure?"

"I think my expenses will be approved."

To Anders it was light-hearted, the kind of amusing throw-away line that any of his staff would normally enjoy, but Zhao took it seriously, as if it were the permission he needed.

"In that case, thank you," he said.

Then, a little self-consciously, he rose and headed over to the buffet table, a magnificent spread which stretched the entire length of one side to accommodate an expanse of western and local dishes, from the raisin oatmeal at one end all the way along to a giant bowl of congee at the other.

Meanwhile, Anders continued with his newspaper until Huang himself showed up, an expansive figure who ambled across the restaurant in his kitsch tracksuit as if he owned this property along with all the rest. Fortunately, his arrival coincided with Zhao's return to the table, thereby enabling a conversation between the pair of unilingual executives.

The welcoming handshake was hearty, with no apology for late arrival from Huang and none expected by Anders. They'd known each other a long time.

"Is this how we're dressing today?" said Anders. "If I'd known, I'd have done the same."

At this, Huang looked questioningly at Zhao and waited for the translation, then roared with his own version of laughter once he'd received it. There was always this time shift in their dialogue but in the tradition of transnational friendship, they never allowed the speed of interpretation to interrupt the essence of what they were saying to each other.

"Don't worry," replied Huang. "My man is outside with my other clothes. I'll get changed before we leave."

"Into what? A *red* tracksuit?" said Anders.

Considering their destination this morning, the Great Hall of the People, this was even more hilarious to Huang and he laughed so hard he had tears in his eyes. To wipe them, he hauled out a white handkerchief, neatly decorated with his company logo, the same prowling cheetah that was featured on almost everything he wore. Originally, the artwork was unashamedly modeled on the famous European big cat trademark but it had since gained considerably more recognition in its own right, at least over here in this market.

While Huang made himself comfortable at the table, Anders told the overly polite Zhao to go ahead and eat. "And please, ask Mr. Huang if he or his man would like anything. Tell him we have time. We're still waiting for Ms. Tse."

On hearing this, Huang raised his hands in the air and clapped loudly like a sultan, causing most of the diners to look around as a tall, dark-suited bodyguard entered. The man looked fit and capable but his boss had no problem sending him off on the menial task of filling a couple of plates, a command he obeyed with just a nod. Then Huang helped himself to coffee from the pot on the table, slurping it with much noise and satisfaction.

"So, Anders, my friend, what's happening in your life?"

Zhao was obliged to continue translating back and forth, even as he tried to eat.

"Same as always," replied Anders. "Just trying to make more money over here than I'm obliged to spend."

Once Huang understood, he smiled warily. "You're talking about corruption, I take it," he said, easing back with his cup in his hand and an elbow on the table. "That's all we seem to hear these days. We must clean up the corruption."

"You don't agree?"

"You know how things are in this world, so please tell me, what's the difference between corruption and commission?"

After Zhao had fully explained the sentence, Anders thought for a few moments. These conversations they shared rarely amounted to anything more than pop philosophy, part business lore and part folk wisdom, but he didn't mind. To him, Huang was a character, a piece of the new Chinese landscape, with his combination of provincial foibles, gross eccentricity and instinctive savvy.

"That's a very good question," said Anders eventually.

"Do you have an answer?"

Again, Anders dawdled. If he'd been faced with a formal audience, he might have debated the issue, offered some politically correct nonsense, but with this man he didn't have to pretend. "Corruption, commission . . ." he replied. "Doesn't matter what you call it, the result's the same. Isn't that why you've got all that pollution out there, why people can't breathe? The plant managers just pay the government not to notice."

For a moment, Anders saw his interpreter glance at him, as if questioning the advisability of such a comment, so he said, "Please, translate."

Huang listened but, surprisingly, didn't object to the outspoken opinion or even react very strongly. He just sighed wearily, as if he was tired of hearing about it. "This is the system they created. If they want to change it, they can."

"They can?" said Anders. "How?"

"Lots of ways, if they're serious. But they're not. You know they did a TV show about corruption? It was a joke."

"Yes, I saw it," said Anders, who couldn't disagree with the assessment. It had been nationally billed as a whistle-blowing exposé but to him it was more like a celebration of the high life, featuring lots of mansions and expensive cars, lots of people skiing, sipping champagne and laughing semi-nude in hot tubs. Although the announcer's commentary was derisive, there was really nothing of any substance. "You think it did any good?"

"Of course not, it was entertainment. This is the new trend. When there's a problem, they make a big noise with a TV show to prove they're concerned but in the end, nothing changes. Like I said, they're not serious."

At last, Huang's attendant returned with a waiter's tray loaded with a strange mélange of cuisines from several cultures. A favorite of Huang's, for example, was to have bacon bits from the salad bar sprinkled on top of his tofu. He also liked French baguette but spread thickly with a prawn-flavored paste. Once it was all set out and the nameless bodyguard was seated, the two of them focused in on their plates and the resulting silence gave Anders license to take the call when it came through.

The voice greeting him was female and in his own language. "It's me. I'm stuck."

"Stuck where?"

"Tianjin," replied Tse. "We were diverted."

"Sorry to hear that."

"They're organizing buses, which means it'll be a while before I can get there."

"You're coming by bus? Screw that, take a limo."

"Okay, if I can find one. But it won't make much difference. It's the same road."

"I suppose. All right, we'll have to go in without you. I'll try to leave word at the entrance."

"Give Huang my apologies."

"I'm sure he'll miss you."

"Well, I certainly won't miss *him*," she replied.

As it happened, the last time the two of them met, Huang made a show about lusting after her. He even put his giant arm around her, obliging Tse to wiggle herself away politely when she felt more like shoving an elbow into his ribs.

"Just do your best to make it," said Anders, before ending the call.

The carefully planned day was already turning into a shambles but there was no point worrying about it. Sometimes it seemed as if he spent half his life rearranging his schedule, whether the delays were caused naturally, artificially, or like today's mess, a miserable combination of the two.

TSE 谢

By adopting what she liked to call her VIP, her very important *persona*, Tse had managed to stride confidently through the overwhelmed Tianjin airport and command one of the few Hongqi limousines still available. To drive all the way to Beijing would be horrendously expensive, which was why this service hadn't proven itself more popular, but that was hardly her problem when Anders himself had requested that she do so.

Now here she was, alone in the back with her items spread over the seat next to her: documents, notes, laptop, mobile and purse. Before leaving, she'd sent the liveried chauffeur to pick up a carton of noodles, plus a local cellular chip so she could stay in touch. They'd already found their way out of the city, heading northwest on the S40, also known as the Jing Jintang Expressway—except they weren't moving at express speed. As predicted, the smog had reduced the heavy traffic to a crawl but at least she was reasonably comfortable.

Bordering the highway, the vague patches of countryside were a monochromatic gray, while above, the skies were a strange shade of lemon. Since Tianjin was situated near the coast, the pollution in this vicinity was a little less extreme than in the capital but it was still bad enough and web-based forecasts were predicting that these conditions had settled in across the entire region. It made her wonder how many people would suffer before it was over? How many asthma patients would take their last breath? How many newborns would never take their first?

Why she'd even agreed to come, she didn't know—or at least that's what she told herself. But of course, she knew perfectly well why she'd accepted. It was because Anders had asked her and even though nothing remained in any physical way, there was still something between them that she couldn't describe. She liked to think it was mentorship.

It's what she wanted to believe, because that sounded like a professional syndrome right out of the human resources handbook, but inside she feared it was some kind of compulsion, almost a hypnosis, with him as Svengali and she as his Trilby. He'd asked her to leave London, a life she'd started to enjoy, and take on the role he needed her to play back in the place of her birth, which she'd done all too willingly. Then they'd had that romantic encounter, that improbable fling in Hawaii, and she'd often wondered if that had that been his goal all along.

Was his interest in her that obvious, that trivial? If so, how convenient it must have been when she turned down the chance to continue their relationship due to her own gender preferences.

Yet she could just as easily have said yes to his proposal and what would he have done then? Would he have followed through? Made it long term? Would they now be all set up in some cozy love nest in Mustique, or Bali, or maybe even back in Maui, spending all their vacation time together? And would she now be living that innermost lie, back in her own closet, even as she shared his?

Her eyes were distant, just staring out the side window, as these life-changing thoughts once again chased each other like the squirrels in Stanley Park.

What she neglected to notice was that up front, her driver was becoming ever more impatient at the conditions. The fact that he was on a flat rate meant that each extra hour was losing him money and after a while, he unilaterally decided that he'd had enough.

Without asking her, he chose to ignore all regulations by swerving into the emergency lane in order to speed past the lower order of vehicles, the cheap compact cars and small boxy vans that clogged this and every other highway. It was a trick he'd used before. The vehicle's name, Hongqi, meant "red flag" and this homegrown model had been originally designed and manufactured for use as official transport by Party chiefs, so he simply took advantage of this heritage to give the impression that the passenger he was carrying was perhaps some minister in a hurry. That was why nobody called the police to complain at his unorthodox maneuver. In fact, nobody did anything, because who would ever take the chance of accusing a minister?

As for Tse, she just continued to gaze, because she was still in her own reverie. She didn't criticize the driver, didn't question his actions, nor was she looking when a high-sided truck pulled out into the same illegal lane right in front of them, its anonymous gray paneling hardly visible through the gloom. Perhaps the operator needed to eat or to sleep. It didn't matter his reasons. The result was the same.

She heard the squeal of brakes like a pig being slaughtered, glimpsed the implosion of crashing glass and splintered metal—and then nothing.

LIU 劉

The woman in the ambulance with the odd streak of white hair hadn't yet regained consciousness but from her identity card, the senior paramedic, Liu, knew her name and that she was from Hong Kong. She had contusions and abrasions on her arms, evidently from trying to protect her face in the collision, plus a fractured ankle, and most worrying of all, a subdural hematoma, but he wouldn't know just how serious that was until they could get her back to the facility.

Yet however bad her condition, she was still better off than the limo driver who died instantly, head cracked open like a summer watermelon with his brains cascading out of his skull. It was horrific but it was no rare occurrence and Liu had seen it too many times before to be affected. In his opinion, it was a national tragedy akin to a pandemic, with over fifty thousand fatalities a year.

To combat this outright aversion to road safety, he and some of his colleagues across the country volunteered their time to speak out at offices and factories but it did little good. The number of deaths just kept rising without any sense of justice. He'd seen infants crushed while their parents in the front seats survived without injury. In this particular case, it was the man who initiated the accident, the driver of the panel truck, who'd managed to escape but at least he'd had the decency and the morality to call for the emergency services.

Assigning blame, however, was not the task of the paramedic crew in the ambulance. Their only concern was the patient, which was why they were now traveling at speed along the very same emergency lane, with klaxon blaring and strobe lights flashing through the smog, just in case any other impatient commuter was fool enough to pull out ahead of them.

At one point, a slight bump caused the woman to open her eyes. It was only slight and only for a second but it was enough to give Liu some hope that he wouldn't have yet another tragedy to add to the statistics.

5

That day, we gathered in hope.

SUN 孙

It took time to exit the packed subway station at Tiananmen and none of the four friends traveling together knew what to expect when they emerged onto the street.

Two days ago, on that very first morning of protest, there were only a few dozen, just the people who Sun and a few other ideologues could contact on short notice. They arrived in small groups so as not to attract attention, trying to look for all the world like out-of-town sightseers or maybe class colleagues on a school project. They mingled and chatted and texted and later in the afternoon, as word got out, more arrived.

By the evening there were a few hundred, yet to everyone's surprise, no force came forward to move them out. The guards at the various sites just stood there as ever while the police kept their usual watchful eyes on everyone. As for the militia, they didn't show at all and the few organizers like Sun were beginning to believe that their actions might indeed be officially sanctioned. The speech by the minister of environmental protection had suggested that young people should be vocal against pollution but that was a long way from actively demonstrating, especially in this location which was so replete with significance.

Here, a previous generation of dissidents was brutally attacked for promoting democratic reform, targeted with live ammunition in a mocking repudiation of the name Tiananmen, "heavenly peace." How many died? Dozens? Hundreds? Perhaps thousands? There was never any official report. And would the same happen again? There was no way to predict.

By the second day, yesterday, more people had begun to show up, drawn out by the courage of others in an exponential outburst of confidence. The political calculation was that some in the Politburo were trying to make a point that things needed to change, which, in turn, was taken by those in the square to mean their actions would be tolerated. And so they came, ignoring history, anxious to be a part of this new movement.

The gathering crowds also drew the media, not just the online bloggers like Chen but also the giant *weibo* services, as well as state-owned outlets like *People's Daily*, *Beijing Daily*, CCTV, BTV, Xinhua and many others, with their cameras, microphones and satellite trucks. Celebrity reporters arrived, too, women and men with their perfect hair and teeth, eager to interview so-called leaders, who were equally anxious to avoid them.

One young woman trailed Sun across half the square before he eventually managed to lose her. While he was proud of what was happening, he saw no reason why he or his original few friends should become the focus when the story was about issues that were far more profound.

Beneath the prosperity they inherited from Deng's great leap forward into capitalism, there was a growing dissatisfaction, an increasing consensus that greed had become the general motivator and that something noble had been lost from the nation's soul. To Sun's way of thinking, this was more like a great leap backward. Qualities like honesty, empathy and sense of community had somehow been sacrificed along the way and although there would always be people who tried hard to maintain such values, it was becoming increasingly difficult due to the state's gravity of corruption.

The big question for Sun, as for all of them, was what would happen on this day? It wasn't just whether the numbers would be down as the students headed back to their Monday classes but how the authorities would react with the new dynamic of the National Congress, which was just starting its new session. As always, it was taking place in the Great Hall of the People, a grandiloquent stone edifice situated on the far side of the vast rectangle that was Tiananmen Square.

In so many ways, this entire central core could be termed the soul of the nation, with deep meaning for all Chinese. On this near side, for example, was the massive National Museum, while in the center of the square stood the monument to the revolutionary martyrs, with its ceremonial honor guard and multiple scarlet flags. On the distant right, across the busy Chang An Avenue, was the ancient Forbidden City, home of the great dynasties with its familiar pagoda roofs, while to the left was the principal memorial to the Great Helmsman himself, the Mao mausoleum. Beyond that, but no more than a gray blur on this day, was the sturdy structure of the Zhengyang Gate.

All this was more familiar to Sun than to most because as an undergraduate, he'd chosen heritage architecture as his thesis topic—specifically the harmonization of dynastic and revolutionary styles—and had spent two entire semesters sketching, studying and analyzing these same public spaces. He knew not only the topography of the Tiananmen locale but also its dimensions, elevations and material composition. He'd seen the square at all hours and in all conditions: in the midsummer heat when it was packed with perspiring visitors and in the quiet chill of winter under a covering of light snow. He'd even seen it dim and mysterious during a midnight power outage when the only illumination was the faint moon glow. And on each occasion, its mood seemed to alter, shifting its character according to the circumstance.

Early yesterday, for example, the prevailing attitude had been tense, expectant, yet by nightfall this had changed to become joyous, almost celebratory, as like-minded people saw reason to be together. This morning, however, was different again. After Sun and his friends walked from the subway, they were faced with the square as they'd never seen it before and none of them could figure out quite how to proceed.

The entire area was divided into delineated zones like medieval battle lines. Nearest to them on the east side were huge concrete blocks, laced one to the other with wire like a string of ugly pearls. At either end were horizontal metal barriers, behind each of which stood dozens of helmeted militia carrying long batons and riot screens, while off to one side was a pair of armored vehicles. Then across the square, hardly visible through the murk, was another line of defense, providing a cordon around the Great Hall where the delegates would be arriving. Farther along, closely parked under the walls of the mausoleum, were a dozen more transports, each with a full complement of militia reserves, while next to them, more ominous by far, was a squadron of Norinco tanks, their distinctive shapes just about visible.

All these elements must have arrived in the early hours, Sun estimated, a complex insertion operation under cover of darkness and smog, and for a long while, he just stood there, stymied by this vastly extended security presence.

While he and the other organizers had expected an escalation, none had any forewarning of such overkill, with the growing mass of participants squeezed tightly between the surrounding firepower. Surprisingly, this was a far larger crowd than that of the previous day, perhaps running into the tens of thousands with more constantly arriving, so many that they were spilling out of the square at the corners and by the approach roads, wherever there was a small gap. A few were carrying handwritten signs but most, it seemed to Sun, were brandishing only their mobile phones, which they were using to stay in touch with each other and with updates in general.

On the surface, all seemed peaceful enough. Yet everything inside him screamed that today might just be another disaster waiting to happen, as if nobody had learned anything. When his three friends looked at him, their eyes requesting some kind of guidance, all he could do was shake his head. He had no idea what to tell them.

CHEN 陈

Of the four, Chen was the first to move, his instincts telling him that this was what he'd been waiting for, *hoping* for, ever since he could remember. He was sensitive to the fact that his enthusiasm for such a scene might be considered macabre, like a photographer in a war zone who just keeps shooting when confronted by the horror before him, but Chen couldn't wait to wade in and become involved. His phone had a microphone application for recording eyewitness accounts and he had a couple of extra power packs tucked away in his pocket. He'd come prepared.

Next to him, Chen could feel that Liang was more cautious but he grabbed her hand, smiled encouragingly and urged her forward. For a moment, she turned to look at the others but then realized that her choices were limited. She could go with Chen or she could stay with their colleagues but no doubt they, too, would soon join the throng. A third alternative was to go for tea someplace and wait it all out, while a fourth was simply to turn around and return home.

It took several seconds before she made up her mind, before Chen could convince her that it would be an adventure. He wanted her along on what he was sure would be his own defining moment. The fact that both of them could end up embroiled in catastrophe was a factor in his mind but not necessarily a negative. On the contrary, it was like a spur, obliging him to continue. He couldn't wait to be at the center of it, with Liang right there beside him, watching him accomplish his ambitions on an epic scale, and he was ecstatic when she finally nodded her agreement.

After a quick discussion about when and where to meet up with their friends, Chen and Liang slowly began edging their way into the maelstrom, holding hands so tightly that their perspiration was acting like glue to help the adherence. Since they couldn't go through the barriers, they had to look for a way around, a circuitous route that took them into the center of the Chang An traffic flow, clinging as close as possible to the fence that divided the multilane thoroughfare, with the exhaust smoke and black Diesel fumes adding to the already dense atmosphere.

From here, Chen's intention was to work his way through to the epicenter of the crowd, one interview at a time. He didn't need people's identity, didn't even want to ask them, because that would make them hesitant to speak. All he needed to know was why they were here. He could always invent names later with a byline concession to that effect, which he considered a reasonable and ethical journalistic practice.

In addition to his blog, he also had the idea of using the recordings themselves in a series of podcasts, which meant that they would have to be of sufficient reproduction quality. To this end, his inspiration was to have Liang controlling the device, not only to leave him free to apply his full attention to his subjects but also to give her something meaningful to do, something that would keep her occupied with an essential function in order to remove, or at least reduce the inherent fear. They would be partners in every sense and for Chen, that just added to the exhilaration.

"Don't we want pictures?" she asked him.

"I'd love pictures," he replied, "but I don't think it's such a good idea."

"But there are phones and cameras everywhere. The people, the reporters . . . Everybody's got one. What difference would it make?"

He looked at her and thought about it but in fact, he'd already considered and rejected the idea for the same reason he didn't want names. If images were published of his respondents, the authorities would know exactly who they were through facial recognition software, which they could easily match to the identification records they kept of every individual. It was of real concern and he couldn't be responsible for that kind of betrayal. He'd never be able to forgive himself.

Despite this cautious approach, however, the first interview didn't go too well. The subject was a male in his early twenties from the southeastern district of Chongwen who just shrugged at every question and didn't even bother to remove his mask. He didn't know why he was here, had just followed his friends, didn't really know much about anything, so after trying to obtain a response for far too long, Chen just gave it up as a waste of time.

The second was with a young woman from Xicheng, who was a good deal more forthcoming. In fact, she could hardly stop talking. She was here, she insisted, because she was worried about the fate of all mankind. We only have one planet, she said, and it won't survive if we don't take care of it. Very soon the entire Earth will be using up resources and throwing them away and we'll be submerged in our own garbage. Did they know, she asked Chen and Liang, that entire species were becoming extinct? That the food was being poisoned by chemicals? That global warming was melting the snow caps and the glaciers? That the sea levels were rising and would very soon drown all the coastal cities?

It was all true, she assured them, her voice rising. When asked who or what had spoiled the planet, she was adamant in her belief. It was the Americans, she insisted, and the consumerist culture they championed. First Europe copied them, then Japan and Korea did the same, now China. Soon it would be India, then Africa too. She'd seen it all on a secret video, made by the former US vice president himself, because he had a guilty conscience about what his people had done.

She continued rambling like this for a while but Chen was not at all interested in propaganda. While some of the more general stuff might perhaps be of minor use as filler material to insert between other respondents on a soundtrack, he was a little dismayed to think that this might be the general level of communication.

What he was really seeking was genuine insight, some original thoughts to prove his personal contention that this was a well-versed society, if only people could be allowed to express themselves. Unfortunately, it took many more such recordings and a lot of expended energy before he found a mature, well-dressed woman, maybe in her late thirties or early forties, who was able to articulate a more notable concept—so much so, that it was as if she'd been just waiting to tell someone her story.

She was here, she told Chen, because for many years she'd been the mistress of a politician, a very high-ranking member of the party. He was married of course, so he'd kept her in a lavish apartment and visited her there twice a month. However, the main reason for this setup, she discovered, was not only illicit sex but also real estate and in fact, she was not so much the man's paramour as his janitor, a person who would build his investment's value by maintaining it. This, she told Chen, had given her a unique view of how the nation worked since she was of the opinion that this man, this senior politician, was typical of the ruling mindset.

There were districts, even cities, full of such apartments with people like herself tucked away inside and this was how the nation's new wealth was being spent. While these so-called leaders spewed forth about progress, all they were really doing was thickening their own wallets. Many even had bank accounts outside the country, which she knew because the man who subsidized her confessed as much. And she was convinced that it was this self-interest, this kleptomania at the expense of all else, which was at the heart of all the ills, including the bad air.

It was yet another diatribe but this time, Chen and Liang listened to her with fascination and by the time she was done, they could see some slight moisture in her eyes.

That's right, she admitted, she did sound like a woman scorned. She had her clothes and a little money but the man had kicked her out of the apartment for someone younger and now she'd have to go back to street prostitution—but, she added, that didn't mean she wasn't speaking the truth. Then she did a strange thing. She touched Chen and Liang on the cheek, each of them in turn, before telling them to publish what she'd said, all of it. She didn't care what happened to her anymore and they had her full permission.

By this time, Liang was so emotionally taken with her story that she wanted to keep talking, to keep asking questions, but Chen had all he needed and was just trying to ease her away when they heard a disturbance.

It was some way off, somewhere on the north side of the square near Chang An. Neither of them had enough height to see anything, so Chen decided to use it as an excuse to grab Liang's hand once again and after offering their sincere thanks to the woman, they began to thread a path around the tight clumps of people in order to ease back the way they came. As they struggled, the commotion became louder. It was neither in excitement nor alarm but more like annoyance and as they moved closer, it was apparent that a few were already becoming agitated. There was the sound of vehicles, too, a low grinding noise as gears were changed and motors revved.

Half a minute later, they saw what was causing the problem. It was a column of militia just arriving but they were in the wrong place, right in the middle of the crowd, and were now attempting to nose their way through to where similar transports were parked on the south side. It was obvious they were trying to avoid trouble by the glacial pace of their advance but the crowd was so packed that there was real risk of injury.

"Pictures," Chen said to Liang, suddenly changing his mind. "Lots of pictures."

"Faces?"

Chen thought about it, then made an instant decision to dismiss his own reservations. "Everything," he told her. Perhaps it might be rash but he sensed a story in the making and that he was the only journalist right here on the spot.

The vehicles were getting closer now, creeping toward them, to the point that they could see the young men peering from the windows.

"They're just kids in there," said Chen. "See if you can get *their* faces, too."

They edged forward, getting as near as they could without being trampled, and Liang got busy. She was a good photographer, not professional quality but as capable as any with a phone app, and he trusted her to do the job while he protected her from interference and generally soaked up the scene. He'd need to recall all the details of this moment when he wrote it all up.

WEI 魏

It was the general consensus among Wei's unit that this was all the fault of their police escort, which had brought them through the city without first shutting the roads and clearing the way. It meant that they were the last to arrive at the square and were now surrounded by this cloying mass of people pressing up against the column, causing tension through proximity alone.

Wei glanced around at his young platoon, saw their pale features and he could well understand why they felt vulnerable.

A few outside had already started hammering on the sides of the bus. What if they began rocking it back and forth? What if they set it on fire? While the metallic body was military grade and the glass was supposed to be shatterproof, nobody could foresee what a mob this size might attempt and that was the problem.

Here inside the vehicle, hands were already gripping weapons tightly and if there were sufficient provocation, it might be difficult to prevent a reaction. Wei knew firsthand because he'd seen it before, right here at Tiananmen. He could recall the sense of momentum, the feeling that events were spiraling away from them, out of control. And under such conditions, it never mattered who started the frenzy. It was always the lowest rank of soldiers who were blamed.

That wasn't right to Wei. He, for one, was of the strong conviction that much of the country, the vast majority who lived beyond the tier one megacities, had actually agreed back then with the government's stand. The leadership had ordered the student crackdown, the military had obeyed and the people, the ordinary people like his own family back in Yunnan, had understood. They'd even congratulated him for doing his duty and that had meant a great deal to him.

As a young boy, he'd once almost drowned in the Mingyi River and he could remember those same cousins and uncles wading in after him. They were sturdy people, ruddy from the outdoors, and he could feel the strength in their arms as they stood thigh deep in the waters to lift him out as if he were no more than a sack of soybeans. They resuscitated him by pumping the water from his chest, then wrapped him in a horse blanket and sat him next to a fire right there on the mud bank. When he was up to it, they gave him rice and brewed him tea, and he recalled how safe he felt, how nothing could hurt him while they were around.

They were the backbone of the country, Wei believed, the ones who believed in it, who took pride in it. They were hardworking and they were loyal. It was they who had built this new China, not just with their own rural agriculture but with industry and science, and that's how the nation had grown, how it had gained respect in the world. This was how it had outshone the west, just as it had soared with a dozen cosmonauts already in space. Everybody he knew had cheered when those rockets went up, just as they'd cheered when homegrown athletes dominated the Games.

According to Wei's credo, those heroes were the real China and privately he detested these troublemakers just outside the windows who were blocking the square.

Nevertheless, his orders were to remain passive and that's what his platoon would do—unless, of course, the situation escalated. Then maybe they wouldn't be so passive.

SUN 孙

While Chen and Liang were busy with strangers, Sun and Feng were meeting up with another group, mostly young professionals like themselves, some of whom had helped arrange this demonstration.

Indeed, it was one of them, Qian, who had first introduced Sun to such radical notions as active protest. But it didn't begin like that.

It began with art, because back in high school, that had been Sun's favorite subject. He enjoyed drawing class, took extracurricular lessons in calligraphy and in his spare time shot endless images with the small Japanese camera his parents had given him. He loved playing with light and shade and movement, sometimes tinting the images orange, or lime, or lavender, in order to create his own impressionistic fantasies.

It was just after graduation, during an idyllic summer season before the hard work of university, that his absorption led him to discover the fledgling 798 art colony up in the northeastern sector of the city, not far from the airport expressway. He'd heard about this new avant-garde project from one of the younger teachers and with no school work or assignments, this was the occasion to acquaint himself with its ideas and even to show what he could do. The only way he knew to accomplish this was to wander in one day, just an eager teenager with a slim portfolio of his own work, offer it up for assessment and hopefully gain some useful feedback.

On the afternoon he arrived, the heat was intense. All was still and little was happening, so the few artists who were there seemed glad to ease up for a while, to sit and talk, pleased that this bright, well-mannered youngster was interested enough to ask questions. Eventually, he was invited to leaf through his own pages of sketches, watercolors, photos and architectural concepts, but his natural apprehension was unwarranted because most of the residents who viewed them offered mere compliments and platitudes in order to encourage the boy to pursue and practice.

Only one was more restricted in his praise and that was Qian, who considered each item carefully and tried to be constructive in his critique, commenting on the quality of form and line, on the subtleties of shade and the use of negative space. In the case of the photographic images, however, he was damning. While he found the dynamism had some merit, he refused to hide his intense dislike for the garish color treatment, which to him was too obvious and therefore abhorrent to artistic sensibilities. The words stung but Sun, the student, learned more from Qian than from all the rest and he managed to bury any feelings of discouragement under gratitude for such honesty.

Yet in recalling that first visit, the most vivid memory Sun would keep was of Qian's cage bird, a small brown lark, sitting on its perch and charming all who passed with its continual song. It wasn't unusual to see the species. Unlike sparrows, magpies, or the symbolic crows, these birds had become an auspicious household pet and there were once neighborhood contests to judge which sang the sweetest. What was different about this particular animal, however, was that Qian left its cage permanently open.

If the bird had so wished, it could have departed at any time but didn't—either because it liked its surroundings or, more likely, because it didn't have the confidence to leave. Qian had found it in the gutter, a half-dead fledgling with a damaged foot, and although he'd nursed it back to health by cleaning it up and feeding it milk with a medical dropper, it had never flown since that day. That was why he'd named it Qie, which sounded like his own name but was in fact the Chinese word for penguin, a clever joke that the young Sun enjoyed.

"If you keep a bird in a cage, you're like a jailer guarding a prisoner," Qian said, "but if you let the bird out and he chooses to return home, then you can say he's your friend."

"And what if he never actually leaves home, like this one?" asked Sun.

"Then you can say he's an art student who can't find a job."

This, too, was enormously amusing to Sun but Qian just smiled gently and offered the boy cold tea, which made for a welcome respite.

The rest of that summer, Sun journeyed back and forth across the city to see his new friend and then on throughout his college years, usually on weekends when he needed a break. During that period, he always had it in mind to rent such a place for himself, so that he, too, could work and exhibit just like Qian, but as the pressures of student life gradually took over, he realized that he'd have to make a choice. He couldn't focus on both art and architecture, at least not to his own satisfaction, so he chose the latter.

By this time, their conversations had drifted beyond the aesthetic into other ideals, such as philosophy, sociology, anthropology—until they began, almost without conscious intention, to hone in on liberalization. They spoke of political systems in the US, in Europe and even more relevantly, in super-modern Singapore, which was three quarters ethnic Chinese but had managed to develop a functioning democracy. It wasn't perfect, said Qian, but it was far ahead of anything conceived in Beijing.

The simple question was *why*? Why was it possible in such a minuscule state, nothing but a dot on the map, and not in China? Singapore, too, had once lived under British colonialism. They, too, had been occupied by the Japanese. And with their independence, they too had sought the twin ambitions of progress and harmony. Yet they had taken a different path. The founding father of that nation, Lee, had talked of the "Asian" way but *his* way was far removed from that of Mao or even Deng. Why was that, Qian asked again?

Of course, there was no answer, because such questions were meant to be rhetorical. This wasn't a quiz for Sun as much as an education. He'd never before heard of the Singaporean political system, just as he didn't know about so many other topics they discussed. What he did know, however, was how to listen and this was essentially why Qian was happy enough to expound his views in the privacy of his studio space, surrounded by canvases and easels and the pungent smell of brushes in turpentine, while over on the shelf, Penguin sang his accompaniment.

Then one night, the little bird's clear voice finally gave out.

Sun had never cried for anything in all his years but he sobbed bitterly when that innocent life, which took nothing and offered only pleasure, was finally extinguished.

"It's all right," Qian said with his hand on Sun's shoulder. "We should be content that he died in peace, with his belly full and his spirit free." It was a fine eulogy but what he said next became, for Sun, the real moment of truth. "The question we must ask ourselves is why they don't open the cage for us."

After a while, it became evident to Sun that his good friend was involved in more than just talk. Each week, as it turned out, Qian met with others of like mind, sometimes in teahouses but more often in public parks—wherever they could get together without disturbance. And on one such occasion, Sun was invited along. He'd already joined the architectural firm and was instinctively fearful that he was putting everything in jeopardy by attending but he kept going back again and again.

It wasn't an obsession as much as a necessity, a secret escape for whatever was in his soul. He didn't know if it had been inserted there by Qian and his musings, or if it had already existed and had just been waiting to be released, but he found himself drawn into the midst of these . . . He didn't even know what to call these people because they hadn't yet figured out what to call themselves. Progressives? Reformers? Anarchists? They debated these issues as much as any other without ever reaching unanimity, except to agree that they represented a uniquely secretive *guanxi*, a circle of trust that could never be broken.

Some in the group advocated peaceful means of protest but others claimed that previous attempts at compliance had only been crushed under the tanks. They were of the opinion that force could only be met with the equivalent. There might be legions of armed men in the security forces, they argued, but there were a billion more citizens on the ground and by sheer weight of numbers, they must ultimately succeed.

Naturally, those with calmer, wiser heads like Qian rejected such nonsense outright. To him, numbers meant nothing and he made the analogy of the single American aircraft that, in 1945, had defeated a nation of a hundred million with just nine crewmen and one atomic bomb. It wasn't strictly accurate from a historical perspective since there had been two such bombs but that was of no concern. Nobody contradicted him because Qian had made his point that their best weapon was not violence but principle. And Sun had been the first to endorse it, speaking up as he had never done before in these meetings.

Then, since he'd already begun to vocalize, he related to them the sad tale of his imprisoned elder brother, which they acknowledged by allowing him the time to tell it. Many had such stories, Qian told him afterward. It was why they were all there—also why they were all now here at Tiananmen, on this day of yellow skies, with Sun more than glad to meet up again with his mentor.

On spotting him at the edge of the crowd, he went over to shake the artist's hand vigorously and introduce him to Feng.

"Ah, a lawyer," said Qian in that laconic way of his. "I wasn't sure we had any law."

Feng didn't lack confidence and would normally have been quick to her own defense but on this occasion she just shrugged off the comment, no doubt in recognition of the obvious dangers that were all around them.

As if to prove the point, Sun was at that moment receiving a text from Chen to inform them of a new sequence of events on the other side of the square where something was happening. That was when the small circle of organizers decided to split. While some remained to fulfill their plan of checking which of the delegates now arriving at the Great Hall bothered to acknowledge their protests, the rest, including Sun and Feng, began to edge their way over to try to quell any potential problems.

But it was slow going through the thickening crowds and the more they were delayed, the more their anxiety was rising.

QIAN 钱

This was the situation that Qian had feared the most. He'd always worried that these protests might get out of hand but the threat hadn't been enough to dissuade him.

Now, however, as he was trying to forge his way through, he was having doubts about his own resolve. Although the decision had been taken by the group as a whole, a true democratic vote, he was aware that if this ended up as a sequel to 1989, he would personally bear a heavy burden and he wasn't certain he'd be able to live with that. While he'd never married, never had children, he worried about those in the crowd who did have families. If this went wrong, they would be affected on a greater scale than just bullets, with all manner of reprisals to their loved ones, including job dismissals, financial penalties and even, as with Sun's innocent brother, the atrocities of incarceration.

As if that were not enough, an even more profound cause for his unease came from deep within his own psyche. The positivity he'd felt staging these protests stemmed from the need to compensate, he was certain, for his own loss of integrity since those sublime days at 798.

In more recent times, that project—which began as a genuinely innovative movement inside an old East German factory—had become just another designated tourist attraction with bus tours and souvenir stores. As a result, many of the original artists had left, including Qian, who found it humiliating to be the object of ignorant sightseers who had zero appreciation for his work.

His ideal option at the time would have been to exhibit and possibly sell his artwork in the exclusive galleries of Shanghai or Hong Kong but he was unable to make any headway. Whether it was from lack of talent or lack of influence, he wasn't sure, but the resulting poverty was the same. Eventually, weary of the struggle, he accepted a job at one of the many budding design agencies that were opening up which catered to the growing private business sector.

As part of his personal transformation, he'd moved into a modern apartment in a development near Gongti, the Workers' Stadium, a newly gentrified district he knew well. At one time that same neighborhood had been bleak, without features or even streetlights, a destination for intrepid adventurers like himself who wished to visit its secret curiosity—the only authentic burger-and-beer bar in the city, run by an oddball Chicago expatriate called Frank. But that era was long past. With the city's rapid economic expansion, this same district was now replete with fast food outlets, not just American but also Korean, Vietnamese and Thai. And not far away was Sanlitun, famous throughout Beijing as the epicenter of shopping and nightlife, a thousand acres of malls, plazas and clubs for every taste and wallet.

Sadly, this hyper-commercial warren was now the haunt of the former artist, Qian, who also found himself surrendering to the new world of materialism. These days he wore his hair long, smoked endless e-cigarettes and slept with girls who were barely legal age. And in reaction to what he'd become, he also drank too much, his conscience pining for the artistic integrity that he'd lost. It was also why he still maintained this *guanxi* of enlightened friends and continued attending the clandestine meetings, clinging to the cause with an almost desperate intensity because his intellect had nothing else left to nourish it.

At this low point in his life, Qian could at least count on the unfaltering support of Sun, the boy who'd grown into a man right in front of him. And now, as they made their way across the packed square, he was glad for that reassuring presence next to him. In some ways, it was Sun graduating as an architect that had helped convince Qian to make his own change to a more prosperous lifestyle. His only regret was that he couldn't seem to accept it with as much grace.

In truth, he was even a little envious, just as he was of the relationship that Sun appeared to enjoy with this lawyer who was with him today, Feng. She was not only attractive but seemed intelligent and capable, making Qian wonder why he, too, hadn't found such a partner in life, a worthy companion instead of his own pathetic chase after all those endless teens who wriggled and giggled their way through adolescent sex.

He felt as if he'd drifted backward, not forward, as if he were trying to walk up the down escalator in one of those Sanlitun malls, and he told himself that if he managed to survive today's events, however it all turned out, he would definitely set about improving his life.

FENG 封

It was evident to Feng that Qian's comment about there being no law in China was just a casual remark, not meant as a personal insult, but it still wounded her as such quips invariably did and she continued to dwell on it even as she followed her friends across the square.

The *weiquan* movement to which she unofficially belonged involved only a tiny percentage of lawyers, concerned as it was with matters of individual rights, and since they all took substantial risk to represent such cases, she felt it was unfair, even in jest, to group them among the majority of legals, whose main guiding priority was merely to appease the Party in all matters.

The problem was that, generally speaking, Qian was right. While it could be argued that there had always been law in China in the broadest sense of crime and punishment, it was also true that there had never really been any solid foundation, since judicial decisions were always subjugated to whoever was in power. That's how it had been under the emperors and it was still the case today.

Unlike in the US, where the constitution was the rock on which all else rested, the modern Chinese equivalent, rewritten during the Deng era, was just one aspect of the legal pyramid, at the top of which sat the Party and its almighty Politburo. As for the rest, it was just a patchwork of statutes designed for specific short-term interests which either overlapped or contradicted each other, thereby making the logical western concept of precedent impossible. In addition to all of that was the morass of corrupt and often bickering administrative levels, from national to provincial to municipal, in which jurisdictions became the fiefdoms of Party-appointed judges and their symbiotic affiliations.

Trying to wade through all of this by any individual counsel was next to hopeless, as Feng had already learned from her own experience. Nor was it helped by frequent citations of contempt handed down to the lawyers themselves along with the sentencing of their clients. This ranged from fines to prison terms, or in some extreme cases, the death penalty. And since there was already more capital punishment in China than in all the rest of the world combined, a few more added to that list caused no scandal, no outcry at all, even if they were members of the legal profession. It was just too regular an occurrence.

In essence, it was also why Sun's brother was still languishing in prison, despite Feng's personal attention. She'd pushed as hard as she could and was simply unable to achieve any more on his behalf without doing irreparable harm to herself. To a great extent, this was why she was here now, as a show of support to Sun, a way to make up for what she'd failed to accomplish for him professionally. As a reason, it verged on the nonsensical and could potentially land her in the very trouble she was trying to avoid but at least the sheer size of the crowd gave her some protection. More than that, it offered her some measure of reassurance that she wasn't so alone in what often felt like a thankless struggle against the weight of the system.

Even her parents opposed her and she could still recall one occasion when her cardiologist father became enraged. He told her to grow up, to stop making a public nuisance of herself before she brought down the whole family. Her mother, the teacher, was more progressive and therefore more sympathetic but even she said her husband had a point.

Of anyone, Feng felt that only Sun really understood her and she moved closer to him, linking her arm in his so as not to get separated in the crowds.

SUN 孙

He loved to feel Feng next to him. He especially liked it in the evenings when they undressed and snuggled to watch videos together but he even liked it on weekends when they went ballroom dancing, a recent craze of hers, because she liked to wear backless gowns and sensual perfume.

Out here though, in the reality of packed Tiananmen, with the air clogging their lungs and the danger of flashpoint all around, he wasn't so sure he favored her proximity and for her own sake, he was starting to regret the decision to invite her along.

As they plowed their slow way forward, he tried to prepare himself for any eventuality but it was difficult. The noise and the tumult were having their effect and his usual steadfast demeanor, built on a deserved reputation of trust and common sense, was beginning to disintegrate. They were in the very center of it and if the worst happened, there'd be little he could think to do.

The only chance would be to grab her and run. If not—if they were blocked, or if they tripped and fell—they might be trampled, or shot, or both.

CHEN 陈

He'd never been more glad to see his friends. To Chen they were like a relief column, here to reinforce the front line, and he shook Sun's hand in thankful welcome.

All were now standing close to that invasive convoy, the militia transports which had been so badly served by their police escort, taking the most congested route into the city and then approaching the square from the north where the throng was at its maximum. All the vehicles were now at a complete standstill due to the multitude surrounding them and some on the square were even reaching up to tap on the bus windows in an effort to communicate with the young soldiers. Others had taken to banging their fists on the metal sides, or kicking at the heavy tires.

"What do you think?" Chen yelled into Sun's ear.

"It seems volatile," Sun replied.

"What should we do?"

"We need to take control of the situation."

"How?"

"I don't know yet."

It was a brief and cryptic exchange but that was typical of Sun when he was in a hesitant frame of mind. Since he couldn't add anything more, he simply excused himself and went into private discussion with the people who accompanied him, including Qian and a couple of others.

As a result, Chen felt a responsibility for the two young women, especially Liang who was not as strong as Feng and probably less able to defend herself. He didn't want to shirk the duty but what he really needed was to get on with his task, to interview the people all around him, to record their hopes and especially their fears.

Even more than the activists, he would have liked to talk to some of the soldiers on the bus to comprehend *their* point of view, to find out what *they* thought about all this. As he'd already learned, the way the military worked was to send recruits to opposite ends of the country in case of situations like this, a method of ensuring loyalty. Should the order come down, they'd have far less compunction about taking action against strangers with different cultures than with people from their own vicinity. Thus, a boy from Beijing might be sent south to serve in Guizhou, or north to Jilin, and these wary kids in the bus had probably been transferred to the capital from some remote town in Hunan, or Qinghai, or Zhejiang.

No doubt they would also have been brought up in their own dialect, incomprehensible in the rest of the country, which made communication even more difficult. While literacy rates were relatively high and everyone could read the same characters, pronunciation was often so different that the spoken language was unique in each locality and one of the first tasks of the military was to raise the language skills of their raw recruits to a minimum level of standard Chinese, at least enough to function at the most basic level. In this way, they accomplished not one but two goals: first, to mold these disparate individuals together into an efficient unit, but perhaps more meaningfully, to develop a camaraderie in which their deepest allegiance was effectively transposed from people and places to uniform and regiment.

From the line of nervous faces that Chen saw behind the glass that morning, he recognized certain regional and ethnic differences—from the flatter features of the northeast to the deeper complexions of the southwest—but what were they thinking when they looked out at the crowd? Did they see fellow Chinese, colleagues of the same age with whom they could sympathize, or just a rebellious, anonymous mass to be controlled?

In simpler terms, did they view the people in the square as allies or targets? Chen really couldn't tell.

WEI 魏

"Relax! That's an order." The command came from Wei, who was on his feet at the front of the bus, speaking loudly, firmly, to his platoon. "Nothing's going to happen if we just relax."

The crowd was still hammering on the side of the vehicle, a meaningless gesture that would only aggravate the nerves of those on the inside. Like his men, Wei felt helpless and trapped as long as they remained immobile like this, no better than sardines in a can, but he had his duty.

"What are we waiting for?" This voice came from the back, from a young, cheery individual who was popular in the platoon and who could often be seen fooling around in the mess or telling jokes in the barracks. "If we're still here on May Day, maybe we can just join the end of the parade."

The rest of the bus laughed at that but Wei, the veteran corporal, glared back at him. He didn't appreciate insubordination of any kind, yet he personally couldn't help but feel the same way. "That's enough," he said, but it wasn't a recrimination, merely a call to maintain discipline. He was experienced enough to realize that sometimes a little dumb humor could alleviate heavy tension. "Look, I know as much as you do," he added. "We stay here as long as we're told to stay here, so just keep quiet and relax. I won't tell you again."

It was about all he could do and although he sat down to follow his own advice, he was aware that he hadn't really succeeded in changing the mood. There was still an undercurrent of objection, strong enough that if anything *did* occur—if for example somebody outside thought to take a crowbar to the door—then he'd have to decide whether to restrain his men more forcefully or to support them against the rioters. Obviously, the latter would be a more satisfactory option but as he'd already seen once in his life, the consequences would be that much more severe.

6

That day, words were exchanged.

ZHAO 赵

It was an interpreter's task to become invisible. While Zhao was one-on-one with Anders, they were colleagues, maybe even friends in a way. They'd certainly known each other long enough and enjoyed a relationship that went beyond client and resource.

However, now that the dialogue was between two executives who outranked him in every way—by title, by wealth and by status—he was required by professional code of conduct to retreat into the background. As a mere facilitator, he saw his role as no more than a voice in the ether, just a conduit whose only job was to allow the principals to communicate as rapidly and seamlessly as possible. It was a difficult field of work and for those who excelled, like Zhao, the ultimate compliment was when neither participant noticed he was there.

A much-underrated aspect of acting in this capacity was the physical arrangement of bodies. Around a table in the coffee shop, his own placement was relatively easy to organize, just as it was when they were walking toward the lobby, at which time he just tucked himself in behind their adjacent shoulders and spoke gently into their respective ears.

The difficulty began in the car. They'd already decided to abandon the Italian roadster along with Huang's driver-bodyguard in favor of the hotel limo, so the question of who sat where became crucial. On this occasion, Zhao managed to handle the situation with finesse by deliberately holding the front passenger door open for Huang, who was now dressed in the business suit and polished shoes that he rarely wore. Not only would this make it simpler for Zhao to do his job, it would also be appropriate because this particular seat in the car was often regarded as a place of honor in Chinese business circles and therefore would demonstrate the respect that Huang always felt he was owed.

Once they reached the auditorium, however, Zhao figured they would probably be sitting in a straight row of four after Ms. Tse arrived and he still hadn't worked out in his mind how he was going to fulfill his duties. There would be speeches from the podium to translate, as well as comments between the three guests, and he was wondering how he could position himself to accomplish all the tasks.

But that would be something to worry about when they arrived. In the meantime, the conversation was continuing in the automobile, with Huang swiveling his large head around so he could talk to Anders.

"So, tell me," he was saying, "are you still screwing around with that cute Hong Kong woman who's flying in today?"

The phrase he used was in poor taste to American sensibilities and Zhao knew that a direct translation might be highly insulting. He therefore had to weigh honesty with diplomacy so as not to cause offense in his choice of words, an awkward dilemma for anyone in his field.

"Mr. Huang is asking if you're still having a . . . *relationship* . . . with the lady who is due to arrive here."

"I bet that's not what he said," Anders replied with a smile. "That's okay, tell him it finished a long time ago but that it's none of his business."

Zhao repeated the message, which caused Huang to grin broadly, showing an uneven set of teeth.

"Ask Anders if that means the way is clear for *me* to screw her."

Zhao did his best to fulfill the request but in his own way. "Mr. Huang is wondering if it would be suitable for him to . . . *approach* . . . the lady."

"I'm sure that's not what he said, either," said Anders. "Tell the bastard no, absolutely not. Hands off. But tell him nicely."

Zhao did his best. It wasn't the first time he'd been involved in such an exchange and he couldn't allow himself to be anything less than the perfectly polite intermediary, speaking in the most polished Mandarin. "Mr. Anders respectfully suggests that what you're proposing might not be appropriate under the circumstances."

"Is that so? Well damn him to hell," laughed Huang, as he turned back to take a call on his mobile.

Again, Zhao filtered the phrase. "Mr. Huang says it's a pity but he understands."

"Yeah, right," muttered Anders.

They spoke like pubescent schoolboys, thought Zhao, but since it was all within the parameters of friendship, it was critical that he gauge this attitude correctly within the scope of his mandate.

He saw it as a major part of his mission to watch his clients' facial expressions and listen intently in order to understand when such verbal horseplay crossed the line into antipathy and to adjust his tone and phraseology accordingly. There were many historical anecdotes concerning interpreters who had caused diplomatic incidents through the misreading of such interchange and Zhao had worked diligently throughout his career to study the nuances of culture as well as language.

He'd first learned this complex skill in Changchun, between the foreigners and locals at the auto plant, and it had served him well in his subsequent practice, resulting in the kind of assignment he was enjoying today. An invitation to the Great Hall of the People was a rare privilege that he didn't take for granted.

HUANG 黄

The call that Huang was taking in the car was from the executive assistant to his old friend, Shui, the director of sports administration.

It was Shui who had personally provided the guest pass and Shui who was currently demanding, through this factotum of his, that the quarterly schedule of payments should now be monthly. It was bribery, plain and simple, a highly confidential matter that Huang really didn't feel like discussing here in the car. He didn't have to worry about Anders listening in but both the hotel chauffeur next to him and the interpreter, Zhao, in the back seat would no doubt pick up on every word.

"Not now," he said into the device, cupping his hand over the mouthpiece while trying to keep his voice low.

"The director offers his regrets but it was his specific request to conclude this immediately."

"And if I don't wish to do it immediately? What then?"

"Am I to understand that you no longer wish to conduct business with the director?"

"No, that's not it at all. It's just . . ."

"Then we must discuss this now, as the director requests. Let me remind you that all he's looking for is your agreement."

Huang wasn't sure whether to get angry with this lackey or just get it done, because in the end, he couldn't see what all the fuss was about. "Fine, fine," he said with growing impatience. "Quarterly, monthly, whatever he wants."

"Excellent, so I can inform the director that as of this time, he can expect a similar figure on a monthly basis?"

There was a lengthy pause as the careful phrasing at last registered with Huang. "Wait just a minute. Did I hear you right? Did you say a similar figure? A *similar* figure?"

"Is there a problem?"

Huang glanced around, not sure whether his noisy whispers were being overheard, but at this point he didn't care. This was serious. "Are you telling me he wants the same quarterly amount *every month?*"

"I thought you understood that."

"Three times our agreement? Are you out of your mind? That's outrageous."

"Is that the message you wish me to give the director?"

"I have a stronger message if you like."

"Excuse me?"

Huang hesitated, just long enough to reconsider. "Tell him . . . Tell him I'll contact him tomorrow. We'll talk about it."

"I'm sorry. As I mentioned, he would like an answer immediately."

"And if I refuse?"

"Well, that's your prerogative of course. But the director made it very clear that if your answer is negative, then you should consider your attendance today cancelled."

"Cancelled? He'll make me look like a fool. I told everybody I was coming."

"More importantly, all communication with this office will be terminated and all agreements you might currently have with this ministry will be promptly annulled."

"Is this a joke?"

"No, I can assure you it's not."

"Why is he doing this? We've been friends for years."

"I'm just delivering the request."

"So why am I even talking to you? Enough. Tell him I'll call him tomorrow."

With that, Huang stabbed his finger at the phone to shut it off. His face had reddened and in his tantrum, he'd loosened his tie and shirt collar which he felt were too constricting.

"Something wrong?" said Anders from the back of the car.

As soon as the words were translated, Huang attempted to calm himself. "No, no, it's nothing. Just . . . just the frustrations of business." He looked at Zhao. "Tell him that."

Anders nodded when he understood. "Well, I sure know how that feels."

But Huang felt that this American couldn't possibly know what he was going through, or how many people had to be paid in this country simply in order to make any money.

Now here was the top man, Director Shui himself, one of his so-called friends whom he'd known for years and subsidized more than anyone else, demanding three times more. This wasn't just corruption. This was blackmail on a massive scale. And that's when Huang realized that the car was still proceeding. They were still moving through traffic and they'd be arriving at their destination in just a few minutes. If they showed up and entry was refused, the entire world would be there to witness the embarrassment—the leadership, the delegates, even the media—which was exactly what the director must have calculated with this ridiculous game he was playing.

Yet recognizing the action for what it was didn't solve the problem, so with great reluctance, Huang redialed the most recent number and didn't even bother to introduce himself.

"Fine, tell him I agree."

"That's a confirmation?"

"I just said so, didn't I? Now you need to make sure there's no issue when we arrive, do you understand? Tell me you understand."

"I understand."

"I hope so, for your sake."

Again, Huang shut down the call but this time he turned off the phone completely, so as not to be disturbed any further. He was thinking that if nothing else, the agreement he just made would buy him some time and that if necessary, he could always attempt to renegotiate at a later date. Perhaps the director wouldn't always be in such a favorable position but for the moment Huang felt he had no choice, as much as it infuriated him. He had to acquiesce, or very soon he would find he had no business left. If a man like Shui, a former member of the Standing Committee, wanted to ruin someone, he didn't have to try too hard.

That was when Huang turned his head to look at his foreign guest, just to check if any of this had found its way through, but there was no sign at all of comprehension. Nevertheless, he shifted his gaze to Zhao and while he spoke in the softest of tones, he emphasized his intent by using the lowest street slang.

"Not a damn word of this, you hear me? Not even if he asks you directly."

As if to make certain, Huang stared hard at the interpreter, saw him look shaken, and was reasonably satisfied that the substance of the call would remain secure. He knew that for someone like Zhao, the need to obey instructions would have nothing to do with professional courtesy and everything to do with the implied threat. Without access to a functioning legal system, such people felt vulnerable and were therefore easily coerced. It wasn't right, Huang was aware of that, but this was how things were done in China and despite all the silky speeches from the government about a harmonious society, he didn't see this particular dynamic changing any time soon.

ANDERS

Bored with the length of Huang's call, Anders had been focused on trying Tse yet again but he still couldn't raise her. Then, just as he was hanging up, he noticed Huang speaking those last few words of quiet warning to Zhao, so he leaned across to his interpreter.

"What was that all about?" he whispered.

"Mr. Huang has some business issues."

"And?"

"And he was reminding me of their confidential nature."

Anders waited a moment but there was nothing more forthcoming so he just shrugged, deciding that he wasn't too interested anyway.

Besides, he'd seen Huang in this mood before. The son of a bitch had a temper and when things weren't to his satisfaction, he could be an intimidating presence. It had occurred in the provincial city of Wuhan at one of his biannual sales meetings, when a local athlete didn't show up for a public relations appearance and Huang's fury had been something to behold.

These gatherings were not like the usual company rituals as experienced all over the globe. They were vast affairs, held not in a hotel or exhibition hall but in a professional basketball stadium with three thousand or more invited: all of Huang's managers, franchisees and buyers from across the country gathered in one place at one time to purchase their inventory for the coming season.

Around the arena park, flags, banners, logos and slogans welcomed the visitors as they arrived, while inside they were greeted by scores of attractive young women with professionally applied cosmetics, who guided them around extensive glass-fronted displays containing the new merchandise.

The mundane business of selling, however, was not the main purpose of that first day. Instead, the session was dedicated to nothing less than the glory of the enterprise—a high-tech pep rally on a massive scale. Everyone had an assigned seat, either in the stands or down on the court floor, and all were wearing the T-shirts that Huang's company had provided, the color of which depended on the individual's status: orange for retail staff, yellow for franchise managers, green for Huang's corporate staff and security personnel, blue for senior executives and red for the few star guests like Anders and the missing athlete.

The agenda began with Huang's opening remarks, then continued with several videos, all fast-cut to a soundtrack at maximum volume in order to pump up the crowd and get them hyped. Then the real show began, with male and female models parading the new lines as a glitzy show of lasers pulsed to throbbing music based on the styles being shown: punk for sportswear, rap for fashion. Later, there would be a brief presentation by Anders, his words translated as ever by Zhao, followed by special guests from the worlds of athletics and entertainment, brought in at huge expense to offer motivating advice and autograph various items for the prize draw.

However, they didn't get that far, because at the midday break, Huang learned that his most important celebrity, a six-foot-ten center, wouldn't be able to make it. Maybe there had been other problems on that day but whatever the reason, Huang just exploded to the point of violence, physically pushing one of his assistants into a wall and throwing another to the floor by sheer force of momentum as he stormed around the private lunch room. Anders witnessed the tantrum but chose to stay out of it because, like the phone call, it just wasn't his concern.

Afterwards, he learned from Zhao that the athlete even had a legitimate excuse for his absence. Apparently, he was one of the Chinese system's genetic breed, forcibly conceived by the marriage of his exceptionally tall parents, who themselves had been injected with hormones to encourage even further growth. It was an exact copy of the old Soviet method for sports supremacy but now the athlete's father was sick due to the injections he'd received for much of his life, so naturally enough, the son wished to be with him.

For Huang however, that was no excuse. A deal was a deal—and for a full five minutes he showed his displeasure through rage, pounding those enormous fists into every surface he could find, simply because it would mean humiliation when he had to go out there in front of those three thousand people and apologize.

Today's response in the car was hardly in the same category but it served to remind Anders of that occasion. And while he was still in ignorance about the subject of the call, it really didn't matter. This was yet another glimpse of the man with whom he conducted business, as well as a profound insight into power at its most basic, the kind of raw brutality necessary in this society for a provincial naïf like Huang to break into the ranks of the Beijing elite.

SHUI 水

The director of sports administration was ninety-one years old but due to his veneration as a former ranking member of the Zhengzhiju Changwei, the Standing Committee of the Politburo, a body which represented the very apex of the national political structure, he still maintained a small, fifth-floor suite overlooking Tiananmen, just adjacent to the Great Hall.

After his years of exemplary service, Shui had been awarded this lesser position for no other reason than he'd asked for it. He'd always loved sports, having coached the People's Liberation Army badminton team during a military career that began back in the Korean War, long before he'd ever thought about politics, and he felt that this might be a suitable finale to his many decades in public office. When the affectionate state media asked him why he would wish such a position at his time of life, he replied that he was just an old man who cared about the people too much to retire.

Plus, there were also certain advantages to being a respected elder of the party, one of them being that he could more or less go, or not go, wherever he chose. In years past, for example, he would have been obliged to attend the opening session of the National People's Congress but since he was now a mere director, not a minister, he was still sipping tea in his office when his senior assistant of many decades, Yu, knocked and entered. This was the only person outside Shui's own extended family whom he'd ever truly trusted, the only individual he would ever allow to manage his most confidential affairs.

"Huang agreed," said Yu, his pockmarked face expressionless as always.

Shui nodded almost imperceptibly and Yu left quietly, closing the door behind him.

A small-time provincial bully like Huang was the least of Shui's issues today. He had many such "contributors," as he called them, all funneling and laundering their gifts through the casinos of Macao to be deposited in his various offshore accounts, but on this day he had other concerns, far more profound.

As his mind continued to turn over the scenarios and possibilities, he got to his feet, carried his covered mug over to the window and gazed out at the vista of activity in the square. Above, the skies were still bright yellow, offering a strangely alien backdrop to the fluttering red flags he'd been saluting all his life.

He'd always believed in the People's Republic, beginning all the way back with Mao's leadership. To the young Shui, the revolution was glorious and he wished to be a part of the vision it was offering. Back in those early years, he thought power was absolute and struggled to understand its limits, wondering why the Party could not accomplish everything as promised. But then, as he grew older, he came to realize that such a workers' utopia wasn't possible.

That didn't prevent the need to try at every opportunity, so he'd supported the leadership during any number of setbacks: from the xenophobic attitudes, to the attempts at central planning, to the youthful excesses of the Red Guards, to the reeducation and social engineering, to the millions who were worked to death on the communes and in the labor camps. Errors like these were not what anybody had in mind, he told himself, but suffering on a national scale was often the result of radical change. Perhaps it was even necessary, as similar revolutionaries throughout history had discovered. Cromwell, Robespierre, Lenin, Castro . . . All were criticized for their lack of compassion but had nevertheless remained resolute because that was what was required.

In attempting to understand history, Shui had learned that an important part of transformation was experimentation and if that had bad consequences, well, that was just the price society had to pay in order to move forward. In his mind, Mao had done the best he could with his version of Marxist ideology but the people were starving, so Deng had no option but to forgive those previous errors and set a new course toward prosperity. The accepted judgment was that Mao's efforts had been seventy percent good, thirty percent bad, and because Shui agreed with that overall assessment, believed it to be a fair summary, he'd supported Deng, just as he did all those who followed.

Even now there were mistakes, however, and each year there were still thousands of protests all over the country, the only difference being that in these senior years, Shui was less able to forgive. Some tensions were broad-based, where the government had once again tried social engineering on a grand scale just as in Mao's day, migrating hundreds of thousands of mainstream Han Chinese into ethnic areas in a heavy-handed attempt to tilt the racial balance.

Other disputes were at the community level and usually had to do with some local Party boss abusing his limited status to siphon off village funds or redraw land boundaries. Yet instead of removing the official, the state more often than not chose to close ranks by supporting him with a police or militia presence. At such times, they would surround the community, block off the information flow and just deal with it by accusing the activists of disturbing the social peace. Some were sentenced to labor camps, others lined up and shot.

To Shui, all this was unfortunate and unnecessary. He was against stealing from the people, felt it went against all the principles he'd once championed, and he was proud of the fact that he'd never taken anything from the poor—only from people like Huang who had more money than they deserved and needed to be kept in their place. In Shui's opinion, this was not hypocritical but logical, his own personal way to counterbalance the rise of such capitalist oligarchs, to keep the original spirit of communism alive as he'd been trying to do throughout the course of his long life.

He'd tried to appreciate all the problems, tried in his own way to help guide each new chairman, but few had listened and now, as he stood by his window, he was no longer so sure about anything. What good was guidance if it was ignored?

For a while now, he'd been talking about pollution. He believed it was an issue that mattered, something that people could understand, that would lead inexorably to trouble, even riots, if the problems weren't tackled soon, not just here in Beijing but across the nation. Bad air, bad water . . . The land was being rapidly poisoned and there was little he could do to change anything.

The fact that he was respected as a long-standing Party stalwart only meant that his current opposition was tolerated instead of being condemned outright. Any marginal influence he might once have possessed within the Politburo was gone, which was why he'd been immensely encouraged when his former colleague at the Ministry of Environmental Protection decided to call out the youth. They were the bravest segment of any society and Shui was hopeful that, once again, they might lead the way.

As his mind shuffled and sorted these myriad thoughts, he watched the results down in the square from the safety of his office.

It was good to see all those young idealists out there responding but he also knew that there were physical risks attached—as evidenced by the situation that now seemed to be unfolding with that single, stupid column of militia right in the very center of the crowd. He couldn't make out the details through the murk but it looked as if somebody had made a serious error and he was sincerely hoping there would be no confrontation.

Just yesterday, the general had given his word that nothing like this could possibly happen, that the orders to both the militia and the army were to remain passive even if provoked, but Shui knew that despite all the assurances, there were no guarantees.

7

That day, we witnessed the rage.

QIAN 钱

Not far away, a youth of fifteen or sixteen, thin and wild-eyed, had a small brick in his hand and was beginning to hammer at one of the militia transports. Whether the boy had deliberately brought it to use as a weapon or had just found it on some nearby street was unimportant. The fact that he was now using it to strike loudly and repeatedly at the hardened metal was foolish and a cause for concern.

There were several of the protest organizers in close proximity. Qian wasn't even the most senior but nobody was doing anything to resolve the situation and he could sense the tension building around him. Someone had to take responsibility and he could feel a distinct inner voice telling him that this might well be the time to seize the initiative, to retrieve what he'd lost, to reach inside himself and rediscover his own sense of self-worth. He was feeling a dark disappointment with the direction his life had taken and he longed to fill the emptiness.

At one time, it had been his artistic projects which had served that purpose but he'd become disillusioned with mere aesthetics and it was now this more worthwhile cause that had captured his enthusiasm. It was important to him, to everyone around him, which was precisely why he couldn't let the situation deteriorate any further.

Calmly, he walked up to the youth who was still hammering on the side of the bus. "Enough," Qian said to him.

The boy turned to him with an irrational expression of anger. "Get away from me."

"I'm asking you to stop doing that."

"Why? Are you afraid?"

"It's not a question of fear."

"You are, aren't you? You're just old and afraid."

Qian looked at him steadily. "And you're just a child."

The youth was obviously eager to prove himself and he turned to confront Qian, the brick still in his hand, which in turn obliged Sun and a couple of others to step in between them.

That's when Chief Sergeant Guan interrupted them, emerging from the lead vehicle to shove his way through the crowd. "What's happening here?" he demanded, full of his own authority. "You!" he said to the youth. "Put down that object."

From the accent, the youth could tell that the sergeant wasn't from around here and that only seemed to fuel his resentment even further. "Don't give me orders. I'm not one of your zombies."

"What was that? What did you say?" Guan was still alone but not for long because his men were already piling out of the second bus, an entire platoon led by Corporal Wei, ready to take a stand.

"Wei!" yelled the sergeant. "Get back in the bus."

"You're out here alone."

"I can handle it."

But Wei was convinced otherwise and just stood there, glaring at the energized mass surrounding them, daring them to advance by the way he held his assault rifle across his chest.

Guan stared at him but then appeared to make a decision not to enforce his own command. So instead of dealing with Wei, he turned back to the more senior of the potential combatants, the one with the longer hair.

"You, what's *your* name?"

"Qian . . . My name is Qian."

"You're one of the organizers of this . . . this event?"

"One of the them, yes."

"Then you need to control idiots like this." Guan jerked his thumb at the youth, who was still posturing with the brick.

"That's what I was trying to do."

"Try harder, or we'll do it for you. And trust me, you really don't want that."

"None of us wants a problem."

"That's not how I see it."

"We're doing our best."

That was when yet another figure stepped into the small clearing that had formed around them. "Sergeant? Might I have a word with you?"

"Who are you?"

"Chen. I'm a journalist."

"Chen," said Sun, who was just beside Qian, "stay out of this."

"I just want to ask the man a few questions."

"No questions," said Guan.

"Nothing personal, no names," Chen said, attempting to reassure him. "I just want to know a little about your background if I may. It's just for my story . . . you know, your origins, your experience."

"I said no questions."

By this time, the original youngster was becoming more enflamed but he now had a new target for his fury. "We don't need you," he screamed at Chen. "The army wants to kill us and all you want to do is glorify them."

"That's not true," replied Chen.

But before he could even finish, the brick had swung, crashing with sickening force into the side of his temple, cracking it open, causing his knees to buckle and his body to collapse under its own weight.

The sudden and horrific violence was a shock to all those around and for one brief instant, nothing happened. It was as if the deep, pent-up rage of all the thousands in the square and of all the silent millions beyond had been exposed in one erratic act, one moment of senseless negativity.

Then came Liang's piercing cry, breaking the tension, and before anyone could stop her, she burst through the traumatized group and sank down beside her fallen friend.

The two on the ground were now exposed, completely vulnerable, so Qian took it upon himself to step forward and protect them, even as Liang was hurriedly trying to tend the ugly wound, using her scarf to stem the rivers of dark crimson which were now streaming down his face and forming pools on the pavement. There was little she or anyone else could do. Even with the aid of Sun and Feng who were now kneeling beside her, it seemed as if she was losing the fight to keep him breathing and tears were already flooding her eyes.

She looked around for more assistance but the uniformed contingent was unmoved, with the corporal in particular keeping his eyes and his rifle trained on the overly aggressive youth, his finger hovering ever closer to the trigger.

"Just say the word, Sergeant."

There was a pause while Guan looked back and forth, considering his options, and for a long, fraught moment, it looked as if he could easily be persuaded.

Eventually, he shook his head, just the once. "Stand down, Wei."

"Are you sure?"

"Are you questioning my orders?"

"Should we at least take him into custody?"

Again, the hesitation.

"This isn't our concern," said the sergeant at last. "Get on the radio, tell them what happened. Tell them it was an argument between civilians, that none of us was involved."

SHUI 水

Even with his old army field glasses, it was difficult for Shui to make out what was happening through the tinged smog. He could just about observe the vehicles, the circle of people, the stance of the soldiers, but he couldn't detect what the fuss might be about, or what stage the animosity had reached.

In his own deliberate way, he lifted the cell phone from his pocket and tapped the preprogrammed connection to reach his assistant in the outer office but Yu was already on the phone and it took a minute or so for him to appear in the room.

"They just called me," he said. "Seems like somebody got hurt."

"One of ours?"

"No, some reporter."

"That's not good. Anyone we know?"

"Just a nobody with a blog."

"Can they keep it contained?"

"They tell me they can."

"Does the general know?"

"I don't know. You want me to check?"

"No, that's all right. I'm sure they'll disturb him if they have to."

Yu nodded and left as silently as he arrived.

Already, Shui didn't like the way this was going and considered it yet more proof that nothing was ever perfect, no matter how carefully planned.

Without thinking, he lifted his cup to his lips and took a few wet leaves on his tongue before realizing that he'd already finished his tea. Annoyed with himself at what others might perceive as senility, he spat them back and walked over to sit once again at his desk.

On the shelves behind his chair were his military ribbons, diplomatic souvenirs, state medals and signed photographs, each handsomely framed, as well as his sports trophies, most of which were, like himself, so ancient that they'd become tarnished. Yet all these honors, an entire lifetime of achievement, would count for little if today didn't go as intended.

YU 余

Nobody knew the old man better than his executive assistant and it had been like that ever since Shui had climbed to his state of eminence, first within the Politburo and finally to the Standing Committee. This was the inner sanctum, the very pinnacle of the entire state structure, where the seven members came together in a gyre of competing visions and egos. The climb to such heights hadn't been easy for Shui but once there, he managed to survive by a combination of sagacity and flexibility, ably assisted by Yu who served as both fixer and gatekeeper, a faithful set of eyes and ears who was always careful enough to remember where his self-interest lay.

All those years of dedication had also paid off in a financial sense for Yu, to the extent that he and his wife now had a comfortable lifestyle in a seven-room luxury apartment. When their son, disturbed and rebellious, was arrested for disorderly conduct, it was Shui who freed him from a prison cell on condition that the boy join the Army Corps of Engineers. Here, after a difficult start, the study and discipline turned out to be the making of him, eventually resulting in graduation from the capital's prestigious university of technology, Bei Gong Da, with an excellent junior position opening up at the Ministry of Communications, thanks once again to Shui.

Naturally, Yu and his wife were immensely appreciative, just as they'd always been for everything the old man had done. At this stage of their lives, they had all they needed, in fact more than a modest couple could ever have dreamed, and yet Yu was deeply troubled. Everything they'd accomplished, their lifestyle and perhaps even their personal freedom, was now being placed in jeopardy by this latest adventure on which Shui had embarked. Even with all of Yu's years of trust and fealty, he was dubious of the outcome and his worries appeared to be confirmed when the news came directly through to him at his desk in the outer office.

"We have an issue," said the voice.

"Tell me."

"That kid, the reporter . . ."

"The one who was injured?"

"He's dead."

"What? Are you sure?"

"Of course I'm sure."

It was not Yu's habit to scream or to curse but at that moment he very much felt like doing so. "What's the situation now?"

"What do you think? It's difficult."

"I meant what's the mood? Any more violence?"

"Not yet but it's minute by minute."

"Did the police arrive?"

"They're trying to get through."

"That won't help."

"No."

"All right, stay in touch."

The call ended and Yu debated how he should tell the old man.

Often in his role as guardian, he kept certain aspects of daily business to himself but only if he decided they were too trivial to bring to the director's attention. This, however, was too critical by far. If this death incensed the crowd, then security would have to react and the whole day could start to unravel.

QIAN 钱

Within minutes, anyone in the square with a phone—which was almost everyone—had received a message to say that an activist was dead. Some told the tale in a brief text, while others offered more exaggeration, making up any details they didn't know. Mostly in these accounts, it was the army that had killed him, some thug wielding a rifle, with a few adding that it was for no reason whatsoever.

The problem was that nobody really knew what to do with the information, torn as they were between two extremes: to run for refuge, or to remain and challenge. As a result, they were shifting without direction, milling without aim, a mass of uncertainty. They'd come to demonstrate against the poisoned environment but now there were other, more immediate priorities.

Yet in reality, no shots had yet been fired and none of the surrounding troops appeared to be on the move. It was a strange situation. Only those closest to the trapped column knew what was really going on and here the main danger was that if a skirmish began in earnest, these people in the center might be trampled in the crush of others pressing forward. Nevertheless, Liang refused to leave Chen, just as Sun and Feng couldn't possibly abandon Liang.

Next to them, Qian was unsure what to do. He felt the increasing pressure, saw the nervous faces of the armed platoon, so he edged his way over to their commander.

"Sergeant?"

The man turned. The expression was tense, the voice clipped. "What do you want?"

"Easy, easy. I just want to help."

"Help how?"

"If you want to avoid trouble . . . You do, don't you?"

"Just say what you have to say."

"Fine. So first, we have to move the body."

"What? Why?"

"If we don't, Chen will become a symbol, a martyr."

Sergeant Guan looked at him, his expression cynical but not dismissive. "Move it where?" he said.

"Inside."

"Inside the bus?"

"It's the only place."

"That's it? That's how we avoid trouble?"

"No, I have another idea. You have some kind of a speaker?"

"A speaker?"

"Some way I can talk to all these people."

The sergeant shrugged, as if it were all a waste of time. Then he seemed to reconsider. "There might be something in the equipment. I'll have to check."

"Good, but first let's deal with Chen." Then, without waiting for agreement, Qian called over to Sun. "We're going to move him inside."

Sun acknowledged but it was Feng who was the first to respond, doing her best to ease Liang out of the way.

Finally, Sergeant Guan, too, recognized the logic. "Wei," he called over to his corporal, "get that corpse in the bus. Four men right now, arms and legs. Don't stare at me, just get it done."

Wei was obviously reluctant but couldn't disobey and after several minutes of struggle, the task was accomplished, with the blood-smeared body of Chen now stretched out in an unseemly manner along the aisle between the metal seats.

Liang was also in the vehicle, glad to be away from the throng but unable to stop the wellspring of tears, and Feng was still with her, arm around her shoulder, trying to comfort her as best she could. Sun remained outside with Qian, who now had to organize the second stage, a far more daunting affair.

SUN 孙

For the briefest moment, Sun looked at his mentor and was awestruck by the man's courage. Qian was an artist, nothing more, a soul so sensitive that he once nursed an injured fledgling back to health. He had no service experience, no field training, yet here he was, taking charge of the despised militia. They were obeying his orders, too, digging into their vehicle's hold for the standard supply kit which hadn't been opened in years. Included was a first aid box—too late now for Chen—as well as the portable megaphone demanded by Qian, plus a rope ladder, which they unfurled and fastened to the side of the vehicle. Once everything was prepared, two of the soldiers held the rungs taut so that Qian could climb, slowly, tentatively, up to the roof.

Sun just stood back and watched, his sadness for Chen tinged with an immense admiration for Qian, but his thoughts were interrupted by the sound of police sirens. They were in the distance, probably coming from somewhere along Chang An, but they seemed to be getting closer.

The noise, however, didn't dissuade Qian, who was now up on top of the bus, legs astride for stability and one arm high in the air to attract attention, an enigmatic figure in black who was only semi-visible to the crowd through the smog. From any kind of distance, he was no more than a smudge against the yellow sky, so it was the long hair more than anything else that proved to the thousands all around that he wasn't actually a member of the military.

Once he felt he had their attention, he lifted the megaphone to his mouth. "Friends," he called out, before clearing his throat and starting again. "Friends, I want to speak to you." Again, he held up an arm, hand extended, as if pleading for the hubbub to subside. "My name is Qian. I helped organize this event today. I'm here to tell you that we don't want any trouble. Not us and not the army. It's true there's been a casualty. That's why I'm here now. That's why I'm asking you to remain calm and everything will be fine. No violence, no problem . . . No violence, no problem . . . Come on, say it with me . . . No violence, no problem . . ."

Below, Sun listened, just as others were listening, but noted that few bothered to repeat the words. It was obviously hard to turn a negative into a battle cry and clearly, some in the crowd might have responded better to a call for *more* belligerence, not less. Nonetheless, he felt that the impromptu address had achieved its goal of making people pause, if only for a moment. But in his opinion, the only real answer was to get this convoy away from the people, away from any possible confrontation.

There would be time to mourn poor Chen later but the urgent need at this point was prevention, especially since those police sirens seemed to getting closer. They were near the square now and Sun was aware that they might be a forewarning, the herald of some new and menacing escalation.

SHUI 水

"Is that a man on top of that bus?" Shui was squinting hard but even with his binoculars to his eyes, it was difficult to make out the details.

"Somebody from the crowd," replied Yu, who'd just arrived next to him. "I'm told he's one of the organizers of the protest."

"What's he saying?"

"Nothing, he's just telling everyone to calm down."

"That's not nothing."

"It is, if nobody's listening."

"Anyone else hurt?"

"No, but we're not done yet. Can you hear that?" Yu couldn't open the window for fear of allowing that nauseous atmosphere to enter but even from this fifth-floor office, they could hear the sirens approaching from the north. "That's the police on their way. Who knows how they'll react?"

In the past, such apprehension might have been about the approach of the military but not on this day. To a great extent, both the army and its militia had remained under control, like dogs on a tight leash, still capable of growling and snapping but restrained from their instinctive attack posture. The police, however, were another matter. They were under city administration and were therefore an unpredictable presence. Shui had all his long-standing contacts in the army, just as he had in the Congress, but he had fewer at city level and none at all within the local police structure. It just hadn't been necessary to develop them, so there was little he could do now to resolve the problem.

"Can't anybody stop them?" Shui said.

"If you recall, the general decided not to involve them."

"I know that, Yu."

"Yes, I'm sorry."

"And it's not what I asked."

"Well, in theory they can be stopped with firepower but I really don't think . . ."

"No, no, of course not. All the same . . ."

They weren't even completing their sentences because all the comments were self-evident and there was nothing much either of them could add. It was the fallout from being here in this office, the frustration of waiting for events to happen instead of directing them. Whatever was about to happen out there, they were powerless to avert it and their anxiety was growing in proportion to their feelings of impotence.

QIAN 钱

On making his way down from the roof of the bus, Qian was immediately surrounded by people anxious to slap his back and applaud his newfound celebrity. It would be a story for them to tell later, a worthy anecdote from a miserable day.

Sun was the first to shake his hand and even Sergeant Guan seemed impressed but Qian was far from pleased with himself. In his mind, he'd already dismissed his own action as nothing more than a stunt, a vainglorious attempt to justify his own presence, a false nobility which made him feel like he was contributing but in the end was of little practical use. He was angry with himself, upset about Chen and embarrassed by his own theatrics, until the door of the vehicle opened slightly and Liang appeared.

With her eyes sore and her cheeks still wet, she attempted a slight nod of appreciation. It was nothing, a tiny gesture, but it meant a great deal to Qian because it was heartfelt. He wanted to step inside, to be with her and to pay quiet respects to Chen but his attention was again diverted by those sirens, as if hearing them for the first time. He tried to peer through the crowd but couldn't make out what was happening and for a moment, he wished he was back up top.

"What's going on?" he asked the sergeant.

"Police," replied Guan.

"They're coming in here?"

"Who knows?"

"How will they get through?"

Guan just looked at him, as if to say he had no answers, that he was just a soldier doing his job, so Qian turned to Sun.

"Anybody texting about the police?"

"Apparently they've stopped at the edge, can't get through, just like the militia here."

"Just as well."

"No, wait . . ." Sun was busy scrolling through the messages that were coming in on his phone. "Might be more serious."

"What now?"

"They're moving forward, something big . . . looks like . . . some are saying it's a water cannon. Think they'll use it?"

Qian didn't reply. He had no idea what the police might do. All he knew was that if they tried to force their way through, with a water cannon or anything else, the crowd might not respond well. There had already been one death in the square today and if there were any exacerbation, it would take more than a megaphone to prevent further loss.

SHUI 水

He was still in his office, still by the window, trying to follow the events as they unfolded but it wasn't easy. There was so much confusion, so much smog.

"You find the general yet?" he said over his shoulder.

Yu was by the desk, his phone still to his ear. "I've been trying for the last few minutes."

"Nothing?"

"Blackout's in effect."

"Maybe that was a mistake."

"Maybe."

"What's all that?" He was pointing toward the northern edge of the crowd, where there were multiple blue lights.

"That would be the police."

"Yu, will you ever stop stating the obvious? I want to know what they're doing."

"Would you like me to go down there myself?"

Shui shook his head. It would serve no purpose for his assistant to get caught up in that mess. "Try the general again," he said, the weariness already beginning to show through.

If this action they were planning today failed, then he'd be finished, his life's work over. Ultimately, all he wanted, all he'd ever wanted, was a better China. It was both as simple and as complex as that. Yet it always seemed as if the more the nation went forward, the faster it was dragged backward: gain economically, lose culturally; gain national pride, lose international respect. And the latest infernal paradox: gain quality of life, lose quality of air. He'd learned much during his career, far more than most, but he didn't understand why it had to be this way.

Part of the problem right now was that he had no one with whom he could talk. Yes, there was always Yu but he was an administrator, as competent and discrete as anyone Shui had ever met, but hardly a sage. Beyond that, there was nobody. And now, just to add to the level of apprehension, the general had selfishly imposed his own blackout.

In truth, the one person Shui really missed at this moment was his wife, deceased for nearly two years now, and as he continued to gaze through the window, his thoughts drifted away, not just into space but back through time.

A novelist of some note, she had always been shrewd when it came to his political career, with a surprising ability to take a step back from his own occasionally myopic view and sum up a state of affairs with uncanny perception. Sometimes, without even being present in the room, she managed to unravel the most hidden motivations. For Shui, she'd been a fine sounding board, a valuable resource, but she was always so much more than that. Inspiration, companion, partner . . . He didn't even have an exact explanation of what she meant to him, probably because there couldn't be just one definition. All he knew was that he missed her badly.

And while he regretted that she couldn't be a part of all this, he also knew the corollary—that if she *had* been here, he might not even have agreed to take part. Perhaps she would have foreseen problems like this and reached the conclusion that it was too ambitious, that it couldn't possibly succeed. Or perhaps . . . perhaps he might not even have tried, simply because she was with him, the joy of her presence being the very barrier to him taking this chance.

It was difficult to weigh, impossible to divine, and he decided to shake himself out of it before he became too maudlin. The day wasn't lost yet.

QIAN 钱

In an unlikely turn of events, it was now Qian's turn to protect the military.

People were recognizing him, cheering him for his brief session atop the transport, as he led Sergeant Guan through the crowd, just the two of them trying to hurry their way toward the police position at the top of the square.

Qian in particular was anxious to get there before they could begin their advance but he couldn't do it alone. He couldn't stop them without the authority of the PLA militia alongside him. It wasn't that he was afraid of the water cannon. On the contrary, he was afraid that it wouldn't have any effect on dispersing the activists, that it would just serve to annoy them and make them resentful enough to rally.

If they were sufficiently angered, they might feel brave enough to provoke the security forces all around them, perhaps even to riot. That in turn would cause a higher level of response, with rubber bullets if the units were so equipped. If not, it would be with live ammunition. Then once more, a generation later, the events of June 4 would be replayed like a recurring nightmare and yet another Tiananmen massacre would be impossible to avoid.

All this played out far too easily in the lucid imagination of the artist, Qian, as he and the reluctant sergeant struggled through. It wasn't easy. Far too many wanted to stop and greet them. Qian tried to nod and smile in return but he just didn't have time for such niceties. Up ahead, he could see that the police unit was just about ready to proceed.

As he arrived in front of the lead vehicle, still panting from the exertion of getting there, he took a stand directly in its path with his hands high and waving. When Guan arrived next to him, Qian took his uniformed arm, too, and raised it, deeming it essential for the police to identify and acknowledge this official presence.

Within a few seconds, the local captain emerged, infuriated. "What's going on here? Who *are* you people?"

It was the man with the stripes on his sleeve who stepped forward and took it upon himself to answer. "Chief Sergeant Class 2 Guan, People's Liberation Army Militia, Capital Division, here to formally request that you to desist from further progress."

The police captain stared at him. "On what grounds?"

"On grounds of national security."

"We received an emergency call, an attack of some sort. We were told to respond."

"Well, it's over now. We took care of it."

Qian recognized that to be a lie, if only because the youth who murdered the journalist, the hothead with the brick in his hand, had simply escaped, fading into the chaos of the moment. But this wasn't the time to contradict the sergeant. There was far too much at stake.

"We heard somebody was dead," the captain was saying.

"We took care of that, too."

"Took care? How? This isn't your jurisdiction."

"All of China is our jurisdiction. And if I tell you we took care of it, then that's what we did."

"And what are we supposed to do?"

"Hold your position here."

"What? On *your* command?"

"If you want a confrontation, go ahead. You won't get far."

The captain wasn't sure how to react. The crowd was all around, some even taking snapshots on their cell phones, and he didn't want to look like he was backing down. Yet he seemed less sure of his own authority when faced with the militia. If he overstepped his boundaries, it might be a fast way to end his career.

"I'll have to check with my superiors."

"Do that. We'll wait here."

As soon as the police officer had retreated into his command vehicle to make the necessary call, Qian stepped forward to congratulate Guan with a tap on the shoulder.

"That was a brave thing to do," he said.

In response Guan just shook his head and remained as taciturn as ever. "I was told to stay passive," he replied, his tone matter-of-fact. "I'm just following orders."

The minutes passed slowly but when the onlookers began to realize that the captain of police had failed to return, that he'd evidently decided to hold his squad in abeyance, the mood changed noticeably from fear to relief. Many were stunned that against all expectations, the military was protecting them and that's how the message went out, relayed as fast as the bandwidth could carry it across the landmark square.

WEI 魏

The long-serving corporal from Yunnan wasn't even sure what his own reaction should be. He'd never been applauded before but that's what was happening as he and his platoon paced their slow way forward on foot, weapons now safely shouldered.

Unlike before, the crowds were now willing to part in front of them, doing their best to edge out of the way, double fingers raised toward them in the ubiquitous "V" sign of peace, while Wei just absorbed the acclaim without expression. It was really all the same to him—shoot or don't shoot, kill or don't kill—but even he had to admit that this made for an unusual experience.

Behind was the bus carrying the young journalist's body and following that was the rest of the column, which was moving, appropriately enough, like a funeral procession. It had been a needless death by any measure but it had somehow achieved this unlikely result of a détente, however tenuous, between opposite sides on this infamous square.

8 *That day, a decision was made.*

XIA 夏

The ranking general sat motionless as the hours and minutes counted down. To all outward appearances he was serene but he really needed a cigarette. Too bad his doctor had banned all tobacco products, asking him what would be the point of anything if he dropped dead tomorrow. It was a valid philosophy for a man of the Tao but it didn't prevent the withdrawal cravings that were plaguing him.

Xia was isolated in his spartan office at the headquarters of the Beijing Military Region in Fengtai, command center for three group armies and home of the capital garrison. In the adjoining building was a coterie of officers with their advanced communications array but in here it was tranquil, with no aides, no political officers and no operational logistics either—not even an update. If he so wished, he could have been in constant touch with activity at Tiananmen, just like Shui, but he chose not to do so. Instead, he'd demanded this blackout period so he could meditate, allowing his mind to drift through its own deepest archives in the ongoing search for validation.

Whether to involve the aging director of sports administration had been a difficult decision. Nobody deserved more respect for his dedication and length of service but nothing could change the fact that the man's best years were behind him and he wouldn't be around much longer. How much time did he have? A year, possibly two? Then again, perhaps it didn't matter. For now, Shui would serve the purpose of political cover and would no doubt enjoy fulfilling his career ambitions. Let him fix the environment, Xia thought, if that's how he wished to spend his time but that was hardly the issue. Taiwan was the issue.

For General Xia, the nation had only fulfilled three-quarters of its historical destiny, with the annexation of Tibet in 1951, Hong Kong in '97 and Macau in '99. But without the breakaway island of Taiwan, still claimed by Beijing as the twenty-third province, he firmly believed that the People's Republic could never be totally complete and all else was meaningless. In Xia's mind, this had to become the focus—not some tiny rocks in the South China Sea, disputed by several nations but of little significance to anybody here on an emotional level.

No, to rally the nation, it had to be the great dream of Taiwan reunification and it had to be now. With the economy already slowing from its former double-digit expansion, he believed that China would never be stronger than today and the men around him, the junta he'd personally assembled, would never be more confident.

As arguably the most famous and outspoken of the current PLA leadership, Xia believed he could claim support from the uniformed contingent of the Central Military Commission, as well as from a majority of the officer class. He was also certain he'd receive approval from mainstream swathes of the population, the ordinary workers from farm and city who took nationalistic pride in the country's achievements. Then, with the added benefit of having Shui on his side, he could probably count on a great many of the nation's eighty million party members. And if the old man was genuine about cleaning up pollution, they might even be able to attract those young urban idealists out there in the square, at least long enough to ease the shock of transition.

In theory, it was a sound plan which could potentially draw in a broad cross-section of society but whether that would be sufficient, he had no real way of knowing. Much of the outcome would depend on how he presented himself in the first few hours, first to the Party, then to the nation. As the face of change, he would become the cynosure of the new leadership. His attitude, his words, his depth of character—all would be analyzed in the most infinitesimal terms and it was for this reason that Xia needed to prepare himself.

It wasn't a question of rehearsal. It was a matter of composure, of aligning his will to the natural flow of the universe, as expounded in the ancient tenets. In essence, Xia believed that he'd been moving toward this day his entire life. It would be the culmination, when all lines of the perspective came together—the self, the people, the state—all three meeting, uniting and evolving as one.

Yet he was also a realist and had no doubt that he and his fellow generals would be accused in certain quarters of conspiracy, counterrevolution and many other indignities, including treason. But that couldn't be helped. The only answer to such criticisms would be to prove themselves worthy of office, deserving of the people's trust, and that was why he'd demanded these last few moments alone, why he'd insisted on this period of personal respite.

However, it wouldn't last much longer. Already in the center of the city, the delegates would be arriving in an endless stream of black cars, the nonpareil of the Party in all their wealth and complacency.

HUANG 黃

The sportswear magnate from Fujian had been labeled an oligarch but the influence he could wield didn't yet match his immense wealth and success. That was the main rationale for today. For Huang, this would be his induction, a debut of sorts, into the sanctum of the establishment and as he stepped from the car at the Great Hall of the People, he was in exuberant mood that not even the harsh air could diminish.

"Look at this place," he said to Anders through Zhao. "They'll all be here, all the Party bosses, all in the same building." Then he couldn't help adding, "Imagine . . . just one bomb." When he saw Zhao look shocked, Huang just laughed loudly, which soon turned into a rasp due to the difficulty of breathing. "Go on, translate. Don't worry. Tell him I understand American humor."

Despite the conditions, Huang was his usual expansive self, greeting others who were just arriving, backslapping those he recognized and handing business cards to those he didn't. "How are you?" he kept saying, followed by "Huang, Fujian." To some he even said, "Fine morning," a joke he'd invented just for the occasion. It might not be the way they do things in polite society but he didn't care. Back in his hometown of Jinjiang, manners were a good deal more casual and he'd deliberately chosen to display pride in his humble origins.

He'd already noted the seething mass of young people on the other side of the barrier but took no pity on either their protest or their cause, believing that all they had to do was work hard, learn the system and they too could do as they wished in life. If they didn't like the weather here, having money would help them escape. Personally, he now had a major plant and five thousand retail stores, with more opening every week, and all it had taken was some visionary thinking, an aggressive attitude and a few tactical payouts shoveled into the right pockets. Nothing to it. The result was a billion dollars and a ticket to the National Congress, with his star continuing to rise.

Vaguely he searched the incoming delegates for his sometime friend, Director Shui, the one whose cohort had so recently squeezed him dry, but he wasn't looking for confrontation because he knew how things worked. The old man had made a proposal at exactly the right moment for maximum effect and he, Huang, had chosen to accept it. He'd been furious for the moment, it was true, but that was over now and he had no qualms, no resentment, no second thoughts. In fact, he'd already made up his mind that if he met Shui here, he would shake the director's hand and they would move on to bigger and better achievements with no end to the optimism.

For a man like Huang, this was the beauty of China: a forceful, directive government that guaranteed a capitalist paradise. In his opinion, it was better in this regard than the United States, better than Europe, better than Japan, Korea, Singapore, or anywhere else, even though he'd never visited any of them. Without question, this was by far the best place on Earth to do business and as a prime beneficiary, he wasn't shy about reveling in his own good fortune.

He had a large villa with a pool and a domestic staff of six, he had several sleek Italian cars and very soon, he would have his new French yacht. And he could also brag of three offspring in defiance of the legal requirement, simply because the only penalty for breaking the one-child law was a fine and he could easily afford to pay it. He loved all of his kids but he liked showing them off just as much because, as with his possessions, they were his status. He even spoke about them to his mistress, a young woman with implant surgery who once confided to him that she, too, would like to be a mother someday, until Huang laughed out loud. There was no way, he said, that he was going to pay for breast enhancements and then let her ruin them with a suckling infant.

ANDERS

While Huang was glad-handing his way around the entrance lobby, Anders remained behind to make a call outside where he thought the reception might be better. This was the third time he'd tried to get through to his vice president for East Asia and each time he'd only been able to reach her voicemail. Mildly annoyed, he tucked his phone away and, with Zhao alongside, hurried after his host.

Before they could reach the door, however, Anders was hailed by a female voice in his own language—but it wasn't Tse. It was a native Mandarin speaker with a very refined accent.

"Excuse me, Mr. Anders. May we speak?"

The woman, whoever she was, had already lowered her filter mask to reveal a pleasant face locked into a white smile. In her hand was a small device which, he could tell from the red light, was already recording their dialogue. Anders glanced at Zhao but since it was evident that she was perfectly at ease in English, the role of an interpreter was unnecessary.

"Have me met?" Anders asked her.

"I am sorry, no. My name is Ren. I am with *China Daily*."

"May I ask how you know my name?"

"Of course, no problem. You are the only western guest today. I was sent here especially to speak with you."

Anders was well traveled but even now, even with all his experience, he found it disturbing when it was brought to his attention that government agencies were taking an interest in his affairs, whether media, security, or anyone else.

In this case, *China Daily* was state-owned, the major English-language organ, and had evolved from a mere translation of the *People's Daily* to a separate division in its own right within the Ministry of Communications, with a full complement of resources. For Anders, it was required reading each morning at his hotel, not so much to seek the news as to note the official government line, since all articles, columns and editorials were carefully screened to reflect the current stance on any issue.

On occasion, however, they chose to add criticism on approved topics but that was merely a calculated gesture to make the propaganda seem like genuine journalism. This year, for example, the negative commentary seemed to be focused on the twin evils of corruption and pollution, yet even knowing this, Anders had to take care when interviewed, as his own public relations team was constantly reminding him.

"I'm afraid I don't have much time," he replied as diplomatically as possible.

"This will not take long. You are from New York, I understand?"

"Yes, that's right."

"Ah, a great city. I had the honor to visit one time. And you are a guest of whom, may I ask?"

Anders was certain she already had the answer, so there was no point in hedging. "I'm here at the invitation of a business associate, Mr. Huang of Fujian, who is a guest of the director of sports administration."

"Mr. Shui."

"That's right."

"Is this your first time at the National People's Congress?"

"Yes, it's a privilege to be here."

"We hope you find it informative. And have you noticed by any chance the protesters on the square?"

"It's hard *not* to notice."

"Yes, you're right. As an American, you have many such protests in your country, do you not?"

Anders felt like saying that protest is exactly what democracy and freedom are all about but he managed to restrain himself. "We have protests, yes, as do all countries."

"I would like to ask, what is your attitude toward these young people?"

"My attitude?"

"Yes, please."

"I'm sorry, that's an internal Chinese matter. I cannot comment."

"Sometimes in your country, your security leaves the protesters, sometimes they move them away. For example, with your Occupy movement. Do you have any thoughts on what *we* should do? I know our readers would be very interested."

Anders smiled crisply at the implied compliment. "Ms. Ren is it?" He saw her nod. "Well, Ms. Ren, as I said, I must decline to answer."

"They are saying our pollution is too bad. Do you agree with them?"

"Pollution is bad anywhere in the world."

"So, you *do* agree with them?"

Anders knew this was dangerous. She'd never dare misquote him because that wasn't the way they operated. Instead, she and her supervisors would simply use his exact words to angle the story depending on the orders of the day and they were experts at doing it.

"I'm sorry, I'm already late," he told her. "Thank you for an excellent interview." He didn't wish to be rude, so he offered her another smile, warmer this time, but before she could say anything further, he hurried off with Zhao as if on urgent business.

"What do you think?" he asked his interpreter.

"She seemed like a nice person."

Anders recognized the diplomatic answer but didn't challenge it. "I should've said no comment and left it at that," he muttered, almost to himself. "I never learn."

ZHAO 赵

As a career interpreter, Zhao disliked being asked for an opinion on any matter of importance. By his vocational ethics, he was there to relay information only, as efficiently as possible, and in theory had nothing at all to add to the content. Occasionally, however, with longtime clients like Anders, he was cast in the role of counselor on matters of culture or behavior, which he tried his best to accomplish in the interests of maintaining a trusted relationship. Yet in doing so, he always felt as if his impartiality was being compromised in some way.

Like any educated citizen, Zhao understood perfectly well how the state media functioned but he was in no position to comment freely about that or any other subject involving the government, so he invariably chose to offer a positive point of view on all topics. On a personal level, he loathed being dishonest with his answers but to ensure his continued livelihood, he had no choice and sincerely hoped that his client understood.

In the same way, he would never think of explaining the proverb about crows that he recalled while driving into the city but now that he was here, right in the center of them, the thought returned to his mind. Was it really true? Were they all equally black? The director of sports administration, for example, the elderly Shui, whom

Anders had mentioned to the journalist from *China Daily*, had a long-established reputation as a man of respect and loyalty. Yet Zhao had overheard Huang's phone outrage in the car concerning bribery to that very same Shui, which had caused Zhao to reassess his evaluation entirely. And if Shui, with all his years of good standing, could be so lacking in basic virtue, what did that say about the rest of them?

Not for the first time did Zhao ask himself whether he was too gullible. He was a college graduate and regarded himself as far from stupid but for some reason, he tended to accept the one-dimensional information as disseminated from on high, just as most of his countrymen did. Maybe, he thought, it was because they simply needed to believe it, needed to believe that the leadership really did have the people at heart because if not, what was the point of Mao's revolution? What was the point of Deng's push for prosperity? What, in fact, was the point of anything? It was a cynical way to think, especially as he was being invited into this hallowed forum, but if these proverbial crows really did have a communal perch, it was right here in this building.

Zhao and his client caught up with Huang in the Golden Hall, which had been refurbished in all its red-carpeted glory for today's use as a general reception area and was now packed with delegates. At least the air was cleaner in here and their sore throats could take some respite. While people mingled and gossiped, waiters in black jackets passed through with large trays of tea, which was very welcome, and the three new arrivals, Huang, Anders and Zhao, took their time to savor it. As it turned out, they weren't as late as they feared they might be, with time having been allotted on this first morning for exactly this kind of welcoming ritual.

"You see that man over there?" said Huang, sipping his beverage noisily while Zhao translated. "That's the minister of environmental protection. He's the one who gave all those young fools out there permission to protest."

"From what I understand," replied Anders, "all he did was encourage people to be vocal. He didn't actually tell them to congregate in the square."

Huang waited to comprehend before offering his contradiction. "That's because you don't really understand China. Here, that's what counts as permission."

"You think it's bad that people protest?"

Huang shrugged. "I wouldn't say it's bad, just useless. They stand out there for days, suffering from the pollution they're complaining about. Where's the sense in that?"

Anders had to admit that Huang had a point. "So you don't think they'll have any effect?"

This time, Huang didn't laugh in his usual loud way. He just offered a gentle smile, at once shrewd and perspicacious. "Like I said, my friend, you don't know China."

Once they'd finished their tea, they followed the delegates through to the Great Auditorium, an amphitheater of space so gigantic it could accommodate ten thousand of these crows in plush, seated comfort. Before them, the broad stage was decorated on the back wall with the circular government seal guarded by five furled flags on each side, while directly above, in the center of the high ceiling, was the glowing communist star. None of this was new to Zhao, who had visited before in a tourist capacity, but neither Anders nor Huang had ever seen it with their own eyes and for a few moments, they just stood there as impressed as anyone else viewing this panorama for the first time.

"Ms. Tse won't be joining us?" Zhao said to his client.

"I've no idea where she is."

"Maybe stuck on the highway. The cellular connection isn't always good out there. Or maybe she just has no battery."

"Maybe," said Anders, as if he'd already thought of that.

It was all Zhao had to offer as a possible reason for her absence but from his own perspective, it actually made his job easier. If Tse had been here, it would have been more awkward since she, too, was not fully proficient in standard Chinese and working for three was a lot more difficult than just two. As it was now, all he'd have to do was sit between Mr. Anders and Mr. Huang, since they couldn't speak directly to each other anyway, and he could handle his job perfectly.

TSE 谢

The woman with the streak of white in her hair woke when they came to change her bandages. She was dazed and showed no recognition in her eyes. She knew neither where she was nor who was attending her.

"Who are you?" she mumbled in English to one of the nurses but there was no response.

It took a major effort on her part before her brain realized it had another language at its disposal and she repeated the same question in her parents' Cantonese but there was still no answer. She seemed to have run out of available options. If she'd been able to concentrate, she might have come up with the words in her limited *putonghua* but that was beyond her capabilities at this moment, so she just closed her eyes and allowed herself to sink gently back into the ether of semi-consciousness.

As yet, she didn't know that because she looked Chinese, she'd been taken to the Tianjin People's Hospital, a unilingual institution, instead of the First Central where there were at least a few on staff who might have understood.

XIA 夏

As the general waited, he continued his meditations, subverting all overt thought so that his mind could enter the fundamental state of awareness that is the Tao essence of life. He believed in what he was doing, visualized it as fulfilling the eternal flow of existence, with himself as the prismatic iconoclast through whom it would happen. He was adrift in time, floating among visions of his career as a way to retrace his path to this moment.

It hadn't been an easy journey.

In the early days, he'd been assigned as liaison to the Soviets, who were arrogant enough to think of themselves as the senior partner within the communist hemisphere. Then he headed up an even more difficult mission to the Vietnamese, who were at that time in a primitive state of development and refused to listen to anybody. Neither task went smoothly but with persistence and fortitude, Xia managed to achieve a certain success, which gave him a bona fide reputation back home as someone who was loyal, reliable and above all, who could handle the deepest of complexities.

As a result, he was transferred to a special unit that had been entrusted to bolster the army's financial reserves at a time when national military budgets were still impoverished. He came up with various schemes, like compulsory lotteries for enlisted men and sales of officer commissions, but the one for which he became idolized, certainly within his own cadre, was his encounter with the Russians—which had nothing at all to do with military liaison and everything to do with street violence.

It happened when the Moscow-based "Mafia," as they came to be known, were expanding their territory eastward into Kazakhstan, Uzbekistan, Kyrgyzstan and Mongolia, encroaching ever farther until they felt ready to vie for the biggest prize of all. They were dealing mainly in drugs, prostitution and ethnic slavery but while highly lucrative, these particular activities all took time to initiate.

In the meantime, to gain a more immediate foothold in each territory, they relied on a surprisingly mainstream commodity: the distribution of bootleg compact discs, which could be sold from any outlet in any back alley and provided an ongoing source of low but steady revenue. It had proven to be a sound strategy for gaining new territory and having already cornered the entire Eurasian market, the Russians thought it would be an equally rapid way into China. What they didn't know, however, was that in this market, it was the People's Liberation Army itself which controlled the illegal CD franchise—yet another of the money-making schemes that Xia had helped to organize.

It meant that when the intruders attempted to hire local muscle to impose their presence in northern areas of Heilongjiang province, beginning with the former Soviet city of Harbin, they were faced with a very different kind of opposition. Instead of finding the usual neighborhood timidity, they came up against a military that could call upon almost unlimited manpower and it was Xia himself who was assigned the task of crushing these foreign-led gangs with their own tactics.

He knew the Russians of old, knew their mindset, so he set up an assault unit, assigning the most physical troops from other battalions, many of whom were the kind of troublemakers that other commanders were glad to transfer. By contrast, Xia welcomed such misfits, disguised them in civilian clothes and sent them out to squalid neighborhoods on the kind of seek-and-destroy missions of which they were more than capable. By granting his thugs free use of clubs and chains, they left the enemy bleeding in the gutters and in the process, Xia turned himself into a popular legend, cheered on by civic authorities and even thanked by hard-pressed local police.

For Xia, this "northern campaign" as he liked to call it had been no more than a minor interlude, a way to make himself useful until the real work materialized, which only happened once the economy began expanding, allowing the military to receive the funding they'd long demanded.

New weapons systems were developed but just as important were the advanced new bases in which to house them and it was in this critical area that Xia was handed a key task—to engineer from scratch a southern command center and submarine facility on the island of Hainan, just off the Zhanjiang peninsula of Guangdong. It took several years but with his organizational skills and innovative mindset, the project turned into a model for the upgraded PLA, on time and on budget, and Xia was duly appointed to the rare and lofty position of full general for his genuine accomplishments and sheer competence.

He'd done well fulfilling those early ambitions, yet it wasn't enough. He couldn't really see the necessity of a powerful military if it wasn't organized toward a definitive goal and in his mind, that could only be the return of Taiwan.

But such a bold result could never be obtained with mere threats. This wasn't like Hong Kong with the British or Macau with the Portuguese, when all it took was pressure. This would take long-term planning and a commitment to ruthless deployment, just as he'd accomplished against the Russians in Harbin, but on a continental scale. It was true there were certain politicians on the island who would be open to such reconciliation but neither the Taipei government nor the Americans who kept them in power would ever condone it—and to challenge the strategic dominance of the US Pacific fleet would be no small undertaking.

ANDERS

As at any large conference, the opening speeches of the National People's Congress were tiresome, just an endless series of platitudes.

Only with the premier's inaugural presentation did it become interesting and for an outsider like Anders, it was notable that there was a great deal more transparency than he was expecting, certainly on domestic issues. Instead of the usual appeal for social harmony, some of the more critical problems were actually being addressed and through Zhao's efficient translation, Anders was able to hear about any number of concerns.

These included urban growth, wealth dichotomy, property pricing, bank stability, internet policing, food safety, labor relations, construction regulations and so forth, with a special emphasis on the need to reduce both pollution and corruption, the major themes as identified in advance by the Politburo and reflected in the media build-up to this occasion.

However, despite the more open attitude, it was clear to Anders that this broad-based introduction was being framed with only the most biased optimism, the prime evidence being the contrast between the hopeful words in the auditorium and the harsh conditions right outside these doors.

Foreign policy was also discussed but on this topic, Anders felt there was even less honesty. While he was aware that the country's main role in much of the world was the acquisition of energy resources and other raw materials, the impression was promoted in this speech that all such bilateral relations were in the spirit of friendship and mutual respect, with tyrannical dictators singled out as visionaries and their tenacious hold on power hailed in each case as enabling their people's march toward freedom.

In this respect, nothing had changed very much from years past, except for one ominous difference. These days, western values were once again being named as the source of all wrongs. The sense of openness that had slowly begun to pervade the national discourse with the rapid growth of the economy was vanishing and there was now a noticeable return to a more traditional communist rhetoric, with democratic concepts directly vilified as a "ticket to hell."

"Are you sure he said that?" whispered Anders.

"Yes," replied Zhao. "That's the literal translation."

Evidently this was yet another form of control, a way to dispel the disruptive ideas seeping in from Hong Kong, as well as from the thousands of mainland citizens who were now traveling to other continents. As a globalist, Anders found this change of direction disturbing and he wondered whether the delegates here today were capable of thinking through all of this for themselves, or whether they were so obliged to follow the Party line that they were able to accept such discourse with blind faith.

ZHAO 赵

The morning session of Congress lasted just two hours but already, Zhao's voice was becoming hoarse, not from work but from having slept all night with the window open and he wished that he'd bothered to stop at a pharmacy to buy throat lozenges.

As he filed out to lunch along with his client, Anders, and their host for the day, Huang, Zhao couldn't help thinking about his young tenants still outside in the square and he hoped they were wearing filter masks.

Of course, what he didn't yet know, because nobody had thought to text him, was that one of them was already dead, not from the bad air but from a brick to the head.

QIAN 钱

By midday, the authorities had taken charge of the body and Qian found himself alone with Liang, who was still very much traumatized. Sun and Feng were off to one side, talking with a group of professional friends, so Qian had taken it upon himself to be responsible for her immediate welfare.

His thought had been to take her somewhere away from the square just to let her calm herself but she refused to leave, saying that what they were doing here was a valuable cause, something that Chen would have wanted. But Qian saw through such insistence as perhaps akin to survivor's guilt, however illogical that might seem. To him, there was nothing she could have done to prevent what happened, nothing at all, but that didn't stop her from thinking that way.

As it was, Qian had already taken the lead by giving the formal witness statement about the incident to the militia command, a civilian's testimony which would be added to that of Sergeant Guan, both to be entered into the log and ultimately filed with the city coroner's office. What to do about the remains was another matter. In Qian's opinion, they should be transferred to Chen's parents to bury or cremate as they saw fit but that decision was out of his hands.

The only outstanding issue was to punish the youthful culprit but the militia had failed to arrest him at the time and none of the crowd had volunteered his identity. He'd disappeared, just faded into the background tumult, and to Qian, the injustice of it all was frustrating. But again, there was little he could do except try to comfort this young woman who was now clinging to him as if he were her savior.

For a while, he was fully involved with this labor of mercy he'd assigned himself. Then the temporary lull was interrupted by a deep rumbling which reverberated across the square before settling into a persistent low throb. Qian searched around in every direction but in the smog and the general mass confusion, it was difficult to make out what was causing it.

SHUI 水

Nothing had yet moved, no final order had yet been given, but inside the building, the director of sports administration was perfectly aware that the noise he could hear even from this distance was being caused by the tank crews who were now aboard their machines, bringing them to life. As a former army man, he knew that initiating the heavy engines in advance was standard protocol because all too often, those unpredictable monsters wouldn't start up at all.

Timing for the action had been planned for the beginning of the afternoon session, after the nation's delegates and their primary staff had finished lunch and were perhaps already a little sleepy. In fact, it was an ongoing joke among those who had to speak at the Congress that if there were good news to announce, it should be scheduled in the morning when everyone would be awake.

If the presentation was less welcome, try to make it in the afternoon because the audience won't be able to hear through their own snoring. That was why the hour had been set according to this psychological schedule at the Great Hall in Beijing, even though similar scenes were being repeated all across the country—the mobilization of key units, with final briefings given in sealed envelopes to the mid-level command.

As far as Shui was concerned, there were still questions concerning which officers would actually obey such orders but perhaps the most unknown components were the political officers within the military, the Party appointees embedded deep inside each regiment whose primary responsibility was to report disloyalty. Xia had assured Shui that his fellow generals knew exactly who they were and on which side they would stand but the director had his doubts, which was why he'd declined to make a public appearance until the day was assured.

He firmly believed caution was warranted and wished to remain as long as possible within the parameters of deniability.

XIA 夏

The adjutant approached softly and without saying a word, touched Xia gently on the shoulder, causing him to emerge from his contemplation.

"Is it time?" the general asked, glancing at the chronometer on his wrist.

"Standing by."

Xia nodded and stood up, trying to shake off the arthritic stiffness he occasionally felt in his limbs, before following the officer across to the special operations center for a final update with his phalanx of senior officers.

He knew that each had agreed to join this extracurricular command for his own reasons but one motivation in particular was common to all. They believed in him—believed as he did that the nation was too timid in its ambitions, believed that every soldier, indeed every citizen who cared for the country, could only agree with their stance. Above all, they believed he had the inner strength to win and they didn't wish to be on the wrong side of history.

All of this he could see now in their eyes, hear in their voices, as they made their various reports. And when they were done, they stood watching him, silently, tentatively, waiting for the order that would set the day in motion. To a man, they were highly conscious that after this there would be no turning back and that's why, for several long seconds, the general hesitated. It wasn't through doubt or lack of conviction but from an inherent understanding of how momentous the decision would be. This was the most profound, most pivotal order he'd ever given and he felt the need to adopt a sense of gravitas commensurate to the occasion.

At last, he took a deep breath and nodded definitively. No other gesture was necessary. Then he quietly stood back to watch the focused intensity as this personally selected core squad went back to work. Once he was satisfied that all was underway, he allowed his adjutant to escort him to the elevator and down to the rear doors, where he was ferried by staff car out to the helipad.

9

That day, we felt the shock.

FENG 封

When she saw the tanks begin to edge out, swiveling on their axes like giant metallic crabs, Feng gripped Sun's sleeve. She wanted to follow them, to bear personal witness to whatever was about to happen, but he was reluctant.

"It's nothing," he said to her far too casually, evidently trying to dismiss the thoughts that were passing through every mind. "They're probably just heading back to base."

"You don't know that."

"I can see they're moving *away* from us, not toward us."

"The point is they're moving and we need to know why."

"The army helped us today, stood firm against the police."

"That wasn't the army. That was the militia."

"Nevertheless, I don't think we should overreact."

"I'm not overreacting. I'm just . . . "

"Curious, I know. Like when you found that film in the vault."

Instinctively, Feng glanced around to check whether anyone had heard, still nervous after all this time.

She was, in fact, one of the few in the square to have seen the iconic footage from those events of 1989. It showed a courageous individual, a lone man in a white shirt facing down an entire column of tanks, attempting to block their way. When they tried to move around him, he just shifted back in front. They turned the other way and he did the same thing. It was an act of immense personal bravery, a foolhardy demonstration of outrage and defiance. Nobody ever knew what happened to that man but a copy of the tape was sent to Feng's law office by an anonymous source, postmarked Beijing. It came in a plain wrapper with a badly-written note from someone hoping it could be useful for anyone demanding justice from that day.

Unfortunately, the firm's partners at the time were too timid to do anything so brash but they did recognize the historical value, so they resealed the envelope and kept it deep within the company vault—which was where Feng unboxed it one day while searching for a missing file. Intrigued by her find, she played it for herself late one night when no one else was around and was so shocked at what she saw that she told nobody, not even her parents who would have been horrified at such a discovery, frantic that their daughter might have been caught watching it.

The only person to whom she'd ever mentioned the film was Sun, only to find that he already knew about it. He'd never viewed it himself, he confessed, but he knew of its existence and was aware, too, that it was infamous across most of the globe, a fact revealed to him by one his firm's foreign associates, a talented young architect from Zurich. Only here in China was it banned apparently. Everywhere else, it was common knowledge.

"Well, all I know," Feng was saying, "is that if it happened once, it can happen again."

"This is a different time, different conditions."

"Maybe, but it's the same place and the same Party in power. And those look to me like the same tanks."

His expression showed some derision. "All tanks look the same."

"Don't make fun of me."

"So what do you want to do? Run after them like a kid chasing a fire truck?"

Feng was uncertain and stood for a few seconds, eyes squinting through the grit as the armored behemoths clanked their ungainly way behind the security barriers toward the Great Hall. It was true, she thought. They didn't seem too menacing. She was about to admit as much to Sun but when she turned back, she saw him already texting his friend Qian to see if anyone knew what was really happening.

QIAN 钱

There were already more messages on Qian's phone than he could manage but he took the time to send a quick text back to Sun to say where he was and suggest they meet up.

He didn't reply directly to the question, however, because he was at a personal loss to explain why the heaviest combat vehicles would be on the move at this time.

Next to him was Liang, still hanging on to his arm after the severity of the morning, while around them stood others from the organizing group. They, too, were trying to cope with queries from all over the square because no one had any new information to offer.

By the time Sun and Feng made their way over, the tanks had come to a full stop, lining up around the Great Hall, barrels all facing outward as if to guard the edifice. But guard against what? Was there a threat of some kind? Had there been some terrorist warning? In recent years, there'd been a suicide attack right here in the city core, for which radicals from Turkistan had claimed responsibility; and not so long ago, further unrest had been reported from Islamic militants in Urumqi, largest city of Xinjiang.

But would any group be bold enough to attempt such violence on this of all days? Nobody had any answers. There was nothing online to signify such an alert, so Qian could only offer his friends an apologetic expression, telling them without words that he, too, was mystified.

"Maybe it's just ceremonial," Feng suggested. "Maybe somebody in there died, somebody important. A heart attack or something."

"Wouldn't we have heard about that by now?" said Qian. "They have phones in there, too. And besides, all the media are inside. I think news like that would probably have emerged by now."

Feng had to concede the point but neither she nor Sun could think of any other scenario.

"Wait here," said Qian eventually. "Keep watch, let me know if anything changes."

"Where are you going?" Liang asked him, suddenly anxious.

"I won't be long. Stay with Feng."

With this, Qian left them and began wading back through the crowd. This time, people weren't cheering him as much as stopping him every few paces to ask their questions but as yet, he had nothing to tell them. All he could do was reassure them in passing that he was trying to figure things out, which was nothing less than the truth.

Eventually, he reached the familiar militia convoy, which had at last taken up its final position exactly where it should have been in the first place. He was searching for his new comrade-in-arms, Sergeant Guan, but the most senior person he could see was Corporal Wei smoking a cigarette with his platoon next to one of the concrete barriers.

"Where's your sergeant?" Qian called over to him.

"Making his report," Wei replied in a bored soldier's monotone.

"And where's that?"

"Not your business."

Qian felt frustrated but had never felt much empathy from the corporal, even when the man's superior was cooperating. Still, he decided to make one last attempt.

"Do you know what's going on here?"

The corporal was reluctant even to acknowledge the question. He just tossed his cigarette down, ground his boot on it, then took his time lighting another.

"Why did the armor move?" Qian asked more forcefully.

Wei stared at him now with some antagonism. "That's the army. I'm militia. How do *I* know what they're doing?"

Qian turned away. This was getting him nowhere and he spent a moment texting back to Sun, saying he'd found nothing new. Within seconds, a return message appeared on the screen to say there was some activity now and that it looked more serious.

SUN 孙

With their friend Qian having become, in just a few hours, the de facto spokesman of the entire activist movement through his impromptu actions and leadership, Sun and Feng decided it might be best to remain in place to monitor what was happening until he made his way back. Besides, they had Liang with them who was still highly distraught after witnessing Chen's savage death right in front of her and was still unable to prevent herself from weeping every few minutes.

They were standing close together behind the barriers, directly opposite the Great Hall, where they were facing all the lines of defense, plus the now stationary row of tanks. It was difficult to make out very much beyond but there seemed to be some activity within the grounds of the building, a line of military transport vehicles slowly approaching the main entrance. These were not militia buses but army personnel carriers, each pausing long enough to disgorge up to a dozen troops in full battle readiness before moving on, thereby stirring a flurry of anxiety among those watching.

Like everyone else, Sun believed this might well be the challenge they'd feared, the violent crackdown, but that worry didn't last long because as each fresh squad arrived, it was immediately directed by senior officers up the stairs and into the building, advancing on the double, assault rifles at the ready. As a result, nobody in the crowd screamed, nobody ran in panic, and Sun could only assume that the calm reaction was because of the complicity demonstrated earlier between the activists and the military—or more exactly, between his mentor, Qian, and that commonsense militia sergeant, Guan, when they managed to quell what might have been an inflammatory situation.

It wasn't that the people in the square had a newfound empathy for the security forces but the earlier tension-stoked fears appeared to have eased enough to maintain a certain stability. The mood of those observing had therefore morphed quickly from dire apprehension into a kind of wary curiosity about what could be happening inside, what the army might be doing with such a sense of urgency and where such a sizeable force had been hiding all this time.

With current conditions in effect, a column like that couldn't possibly have penetrated the congested traffic, nor the immense crowd, and it was Sun himself, knowing the area intimately from his architectural studies, who finally figured out that a unit of that size must have been stationed on the other side of the Great Hall, on the closed-off street called Renda Huitang.

Beyond was an open park with a broad lake, at the center of which stood the National Center for the Performing Arts, a futuristic ellipsoid-shaped edifice built of smooth titanium and glass and known colloquially as the "Egg." Although invisible from here in the square, Sun could easily imagine that there would be more than enough space on the grounds between the two great structures to park an entire division if the army so wished and it would therefore be a simple matter to drive around toward the square within the enclosed defense perimeter.

As Sun explained all this to those around him, he was also keeping an eye on his phone browser because surely, he felt, the media already inside would soon have to report on this sudden intrusion. But before any news could emerge, two things happened: the return of Qian from his fruitless excursion to the militia; and the unexpected arrival of a large army helicopter, hovering over Tiananmen so low they could feel its downdraft.

XIA 夏

The craft hovered but didn't descend on the packed square. Instead, it flew over the Great Hall and landed beyond their view on the other side, alighting on a makeshift area close to where the army had organized its staging point. As it touched down, escort officials hurried to greet it, instinctively bending their heads to avoid the slowing rotors.

After the door swung open and the stairs unfolded, first out was General Xia, pausing to place his peaked cap on his graying head and straighten out his medal-bedecked uniform with its starred epaulets and strings of gold braid. Then he strode slowly across the pavement, his face suitably grave for the occasion.

In his mind, he'd rehearsed this solemn demeanor many times in order to create a deliberate effect—that of a humble public servant who was obliged, while at the same time saddened, to take this necessary step. He would appear benevolent, as if knowing precisely what was required while trying to maintain the utmost restraint, an appearance designed to express responsibility more than to demonstrate power. What he had to avoid was any sense of triumphalism, employing instead a modest attitude as advocated by the Tao philosophy he continually wished to emulate.

He thought he was ready, believed that his preparations had been thorough, but even so, he had little idea how it would all transpire. So far, the first indications were auspicious and he was thankful. All seven regions had reported as ready and in position, each taking up their stance at key administrative offices in strategic cities, while here in the capital, he had additional units ready to control the main Xinhua news agency over in Shijingshan, as well as CCTV close by in Chaoyang.

Even more propitiously, the crowds here in the heart of the city seemed reasonably docile when he circled over Tiananmen. It had been the general's original expectation that such motivation for protest would have faded with the combination of circumstances: the start of the working week, the opening of Congress and the imposition of a heavy security presence, not to mention the bad atmospheric conditions. But on the contrary, their numbers had only grown larger and he decided he had no choice but to allow events to take their course. The plan had been fixed for today and it would have been a far greater risk to postpone the action.

Having made that decision, Xia's biggest concern had been that some small incident, some minor conflict, might erupt in the square and turn a peaceful gathering into a cauldron of rage, necessitating a harsh reaction from either the militia or the police. It would have been distracting, possibly even calamitous, yet that hadn't happened and Xia felt a growing sense of good fortune, not just for himself but for the billion and a half citizens who he genuinely believed were longing for the kind of strong, decisive leadership he could provide.

QIAN 钱

As he'd predicted, word began leaking out of the Great Hall but the facts were still unclear. There were garbled texts from media contacts that talked of an "emergency alert" or "terrorist threat" and for a short while, this was Qian's working assumption: that there had been some kind of intelligence that had triggered the army's response, perhaps some kind of external threat, as happened in New York, with civil airliners deliberately flown into prominent buildings.

As a reason for the heavy deployment, it seemed valid enough, since there could be no better target than the Great Hall of the People, especially when packed with so many party chiefs as it was today. But as Sun argued, if that were the case, why would they be sending armed troops inside? Under such circumstances, wouldn't an orderly evacuation by first responders be more appropriate?

These were questions that couldn't be answered. Yet even as they were trying to figure it out, others monitoring their own news-feed sources began seeing snippets about an armed occupation of the National Congress. One even had the audacity to use the phrase "military coup." That set the group around Qian into a frenzy of chatter until the number and frequency of the bulletins began to slacken. Finally, a few minutes later, the information flow ceased altogether as the entire internet shut down, which only served to fuel more rumors that the vast bureaucracy charged with censoring the web had received some kind of supreme order to that effect.

"Maybe we should go," Feng said quietly.

She was speaking to no one in particular but Sun was the closest and he was the one who replied.

"You mean leave?"

"If we tell people to go, they will. I mean wouldn't that be better? For everyone's safety?"

"If there's hysteria, nobody will be safe."

"Safe? Look at those tanks. Which way are their guns pointing, tell me that?"

Sun couldn't deny it. The long barrels were indeed facing outward toward the crowd but there'd been no further movement and certainly nothing to suggest any direct threat as yet. "We can't leave now," he said, as if dismissing the whole idea.

But Qian, for his part, thought that Feng's caution might indeed have merit, so he intervened with a compromise. "We'll give it a few more minutes," he said, making the decision for all of them. "If we see anything we don't like, we'll send out word to leave as calmly as possible."

"And if they shut down our phones?" Feng said.

"You mean the cell towers?"

"Why not?"

"Then we'll do it the old-fashioned way," Qian replied. "They can't shut down our voices." He said it with an encouraging smile but it was somewhat lacking in sincerity because he was starting to feel that with each passing minute, the risks would only grow.

ANDERS

The heavily armed troops had shut down the media center, informing the assembled journalists and technicians that the action was due to national security, and were now entering the Great Auditorium itself, taking up position on every level, along every aisle and at every exit.

While one platoon stationed itself along the front, another mounted the stairs of the broad stage and took up positions there. In effect, it meant they were now holding the national leadership at gunpoint—the entire Politburo, including the seven members of the Standing Committee—while the rest of the delegates were in a state of stunned silence. A few had retained enough presence of mind to tap out their messages but only until a special detachment began circulating with black plastic sacks, demanding that all mobile devices be given up. Row by row they went, aisle by aisle, and everybody obeyed because nobody knew or could even guess what the consequences of refusal might be.

As for Anders, his instinct as an American was to stand up, to demand an explanation for what this was all about, but he needed Zhao to translate and Zhao was shaking his head, holding his client's arm, asking him to sit down and stay calm. It was evident that the interpreter, too, was astonished by these events but his inclination was to be less reactive and employ more discretion.

Reluctantly, Anders took heed and eased himself back down into his seat. He'd heard Zhao's stories of that day in the past when as a youngster he'd run from the square, bullets all around. Anders had listened and although he could now understand the need for prudence, he chafed at the notion. His adrenaline was flowing, his head was pulsating and he was beginning to feel that this might well be some kind of hostage situation. All his anti-kidnap training as a contemporary global executive was screaming at him, urging him to do something, anything, because the specialists had told him that a crisis like this, once initiated, might only get worse.

He glanced over at Huang, looking for some kind of direction, but contrary to all expectations, the big man wasn't furious. On the contrary, he was almost dormant. He said nothing but his eyes had narrowed slightly, offering the impression that he was attempting to assess the situation, to calculate the odds, to pry apart the reason why this could be taking place at this time, to try to figure out who might be behind it and what they might conceivably be seeking. But whatever Huang was thinking, he wasn't passing it along to anyone else and that left Anders with just one option, which was to take the lead himself.

He began by glancing around but all he could see was increasing restlessness as the frustration grew. He continued looking and checking, left and right, front and back, but if any of the delegates had some precipitate knowledge of these events, they weren't revealing it. As far as Anders could make out, all seemed to be just waiting for something to happen.

The soldiers had already passed, collecting phones on the way so that no one could send a message or receive any news. But Anders was different. He'd dumped his local cell like everyone else, the one with the chip purchased on arrival at the airport, but unlike the others, he also had a second device in his pocket. This was his home-based mobile still on its New York network, the one he didn't normally use in China because the roaming charges were so exorbitant, and it was this he now fingered, waiting for the opportune moment while hoping the battery was sufficiently charged.

But who would he call? The question raced through his brain.

Ideally, he'd text the local US Embassy, a senior contact he knew called Dean who would be his most immediate source of assistance. The problem was that he didn't have the number on this phone's index and it might be dangerous to search for it. If he were spotted, he might be targeted and he was already far too visible as the only westerner present. Failing that, the most obvious option was his old college buddy, Hoyle, who worked for the State Department and with whom Anders had always remained close.

That seemed like the most promising idea but he'd have to wait until he was certain he wouldn't be caught and right now there was a soldier—maybe some kind of NCO—standing no more than twenty yards away with a clear sightline.

As Anders waited, memories of Hoyle came flickering back, especially that infectious grin when they were out on some frat-boy bender, a pair of rogues on the loose, not so much getting into trouble as trying in vain to stay out of it. But that was Hoyle, game for anything, a dilettante when it came to work habits, but with enough charm that he could use his family connections to talk his way into a comfortable niche as attaché to the US diplomatic corps in Berlin—which was where he settled, met a handsome German woman and raised two fine boys.

Sadly though, that charmed life came to a sudden end when his elder son died in an avalanche and after that, nothing was ever the same, neither the casual attitude nor the perfect marriage. Yet through it all, Hoyle remained at his post, as if his job were of some special importance, and one time, it occurred to Anders to ask openly whether the man had any Agency affiliation, some kind of alternative life in intelligence. Of course, the suggestion was dismissed as ludicrous, which only caused Anders to wonder even more.

At any rate, Hoyle's exact status didn't matter at this moment. Whether he was a dutiful attaché or a clandestine operative, the principal requirement was merely that he receive the communication and act accordingly.

Once more, Anders glanced across at the NCO who hadn't yet moved. A full minute passed, then another. Finally, an officer strolled along and the two uniformed men became preoccupied with their own conversation.

It was a chance to act and Anders decided that he had to take it. As surreptitiously as possible, he eased the small rectangle from his pocket, holding it low in order to shield the light and mute the volume before flicking it on. After selecting Hoyle as the recipient, he tapped out a cryptic text—*"coup bj gr8 hall"*—and pressed the send button. He also thought of snapping off a picture but Zhao was already becoming distressed at this subterfuge, so Anders resisted that temptation and tucked the phone back into his pocket.

It was about all he could do.

DEAN

As deputy chief of mission, Dean was deeply engaged in his corner office on the fourth floor of the embassy building, attempting to make sense of the multiple updates. On the desk in front of him was an open laptop and across the room on the adjacent wall was a wide-screen monitor displaying the ongoing broadcast as provided by the government-owned CCTV-1, the nation's primary news channel.

A forty-three-year-old from Michigan, Dean was unusually young for such a responsibility but he'd become a State Department lifer by his cautious approach to just about everything, studying each piece of information through those bifocals he always wore with the same deep intensity. He'd learned his Chinese the same way and although he was by no means fluent, his skills were sufficient that he could continue to work on his PC even as he listened for any breaking television bulletin.

Then, in the early afternoon, both screens went blank in rapid succession. A few moments later, a senior aide appeared at the door.

"They just shut down."

"So I see," said Dean. "How about cell service?"

"Still active for now."

Dean simply nodded. Not much in this world surprised him anymore. "What else you got there?"

"Reports still coming in. But there's one new thing might be of interest. Seems the Agency just got a call from Berlin station, some attaché there called Hoyle. Claims he received a text from an old pal here in BJ named Anders who's being held in the Great Hall."

"Anders . . . Anders . . . Wait, I know that name. Business type, right?"

"So I'm told. Wants to tell the world there's a coup taking place."

"A coup? That's what he said?"

"That was the word he used."

Dean acknowledged this new information but it was no more than he'd already surmised. "Can we reach him at all?"

"We've been trying but no luck yet. If his phone's off, he might not even know we're calling him."

"All right, keep at it. I'll let the boss know."

A couple of minutes later, Dean was entering a far more spacious office, replete with medieval silk prints, temple gongs, abstract marble landscapes and other cultural artifacts. But the woman he called "boss" was still on the phone to DC, facing away from him, so Dean had to be patient.

This was her first ambassadorial post and one of the primary issues she'd faced on arrival was a tense standoff when a dissident took refuge here at the embassy asking for asylum. Negotiating with Chinese security on behalf of the State Department had been an arduous affair, a direct conflict between her professional and personal interests. While State was demanding she preserve the bilateral relationship, her moral values were insisting she defend the man's right to freedom.

In such situations, there's rarely a right answer and eventually the minor crisis was resolved to nobody's real satisfaction when the victim was permitted to emigrate but his immediate family had to stay in the country, which served as insurance for Beijing against any adverse consequences.

At the time, Dean in his role of counselor had been of considerable assistance in helping her to weigh the options and it had built an effective working relationship between them.

At last, she acknowledged his presence and put her hand over the phone.

"Speak," she said.

"We think there's an American inside," he told her.

"You think, or you know?"

"The guy managed to text a friend of his at Berlin station."

"Hostage situation?"

"We're not sure but he seems to be confirming the coup scenario."

The ambassador was still holding the live phone. "Okay," she said, obviously anxious to get back to her long-distance connection. "Anything else?"

"More reports coming in all the time . . . Shenzhen, Chongqing, Nanjing, Qingdao . . ." These were major regional centers where the military had been reported active.

"Do we know who's fronting it yet?"

"Nothing of substance but . . ."

"But?'

"NSA's picking up some chatter about a general called Xia, northern command."

"Xia? Wasn't he the one built the Hainan base? We think this is him?"

"Fits the profile."

"What's the Agency saying?"

"They don't want to commit."

"They never do," said the ambassador before swiveling back to resume her conversation with State. The meeting was over and it seemed as if Dean had been dismissed.

He'd been stationed here in Beijing for six years now, very much the veteran of the embassy in terms of practical experience, and in all that time nothing of this scope had ever been raised, even as a possibility. A coup d'état? In the context of China, this could be deemed a truly extraordinary event, almost unimaginable, and all he could think was that it must have taken an exceptional degree of planning, not to mention courage.

While it made sense to him that they'd launch such a move on the first day of the National Congress as a way to catch the entire Party leadership in one place at one time, it was less evident why they'd do it when Tiananmen was full of young activists—but that gave him another thought and on the way back to his own office, he stopped by his aide's desk.

"Who's in the square right now?" he demanded.

"Couple from upstairs, dressed as tourists."

The concept of "upstairs" was internal jargon, referring to the sizeable contingent of CIA personnel on the top two floors.

"Any of ours?" asked Dean, meaning his own department staffers.

"No, but I think Cai might be down there someplace."

"Cai? All right, good." Cai was Taiwanese, no longer working at the embassy but still a useful asset. "Do me a favor, ask him to track down whoever's running the protest, find out what *they* know."

CAI 蔡

Some people tend to be outcasts due to nothing but their physical appearance and that was certainly how Cai felt. From a young age, his skin had been mottled with pale, almost white patches that medical specialists said were caused by an untreatable syndrome known as vitiligo. It wasn't in any way contagious, it was merely a pigment discoloration but it had made Cai self-conscious ever since he first looked in a mirror and he'd grown involuntarily into an eternal man of the shadows, as invisible as possible yet aware of everything.

As such, he'd seen most of what had already happened on this day. He was there when the militia convoy came to a standstill in the crowd, when the youth struck the journalist and when some long-haired activist mounted a vehicle to speak. He'd then followed as that same individual accompanied the militia sergeant to face down the police. After that, he'd watched the tanks move, the troops arrive, the helicopter descend—and had already made an educated guess about which general was inside the craft because he made it his business to be aware of such things.

An exile from Taiwan, Cai regarded himself as something of an alien here in Beijing and not just because of his complexion.

Back home in Taipei, there were in fact two ideological camps: the majority, who enjoyed their democratic, consumerist lifestyle and saw American support as a necessary evil; and the minority, who continued to believe that their manifest destiny was to reunite with Beijing and it was to this latter faction that Cai's father had dedicated his life. He was a politician in that breakaway island's legislature and was both personally and publically committed to rejoining the mainland. Such people were constantly reaching out, sometimes legally but also in secret, to like-minded people across the straits—people like General Xia, who once met with a delegation led by Cai's father at a covert offshore location.

Naturally, Cai had been encouraged to emulate his father. He'd enjoyed a comfortable childhood and had received an excellent education in Chinese humanities at the exclusive Academia Sinica. Many of his friends, however, had been accepted at the more mainstream National University just across town and he found their more contemporary arguments compelling. By their rationale, the free citizens of Taiwan were not Chinese but Taiwanese.

They spoke the same language—albeit tinted by their own Min Nan dialect—but for them, ethnicity was not the same as nationality. Instead of believing that they were some small offshore island that had been disconnected from the mainland by war and revolution, they preferred to think of themselves as citizens of the modern world, more in keeping with the likes of Singapore and South Korea, which had grown and prospered independently by their own smart policies and entrepreneurial spirit.

For years, Cai kept these private thoughts to himself until one weekend, a few weeks after his graduation, a minor war broke out in the family kitchen with his father furious at being defied, even calling his own son a freak—a *freak*—because of that skin coloration, and Cai's mother trying to protect her dinnerware from being thrown across the table. Neither of the males was willing to yield, so that's how they parted, with Cai hugging his mother before slamming the door and leaving the house forever. Even now, even in his early thirties, the screaming of that day still rang in his ears, the raw memories of the insult an unhealed scar on his psyche.

Cut off from all family funds, Cai was obliged to abandon his studies and ask for lodging with his older sister and her family. Without a degree, life was difficult and demeaning, until a school

friend recommended him for a job as a driver at the American In-
stitute, for which he was grateful but immensely over-qualified.

This quasi-consulate, ostensibly private, was set up as a convenience to serve US interests without unduly annoying Beijing,
which had never recognized the island's government. As such, it
had also become a recruitment center and training facility for potential covert operatives, a program that Cai was invited to join after someone on staff realized the young man's intellect and potential.

Initially, it sounded to Cai like a more ambitious career choice
than driving, so he agreed but later, with the maturity of hindsight,
he began to understand that he'd been more interested in the act of
silent rebellion against his father than engaging in stealth activities
under the auspices of a superpower.

That realization, however, didn't occur until after he'd been
transferred on assignment to Beijing and had spent a couple of
years working with the Central Intelligence Agency as a junior analyst. Only when he'd managed to figure out his own motivations
did he leave American government service to join a private security corporation, a high-powered domestic firm that was licensed by
the authorities to provide a personalized service to Chinese executives and which offered him a financial package several times greater than he'd been making at the embassy.

It was a better deal in so many respects, yet he chose to keep
his options open by maintaining discrete contact with his former
employers and by even accepting the occasional freelance assignment—not for the clandestine Agency this time but for Dean and
his people, whenever they needed some inside information they
couldn't obtain by other methods.

It was in this context that the request filtered through, encrypt-
ed within a normal text message. It seemed they wanted him to ask
the crowd organizers what was happening, a harmless enough task,
and his thoughts immediately turned to the young man with the
long hair who'd climbed on top of the bus. But it would take a while
to find him among all the thousands and besides, he knew a great
deal more than any protester, so why bother?

Instead of wasting time in a pointless search, he therefore found his way south of the square to a narrow alley off Meishi Lu where he'd parked his beloved motorcycle. The machine was a Japanese model, powerful enough to be quick but slim enough to negotiate between traffic lanes, and he used it far more than the SUV his company had leased for him, which was now semi-permanently parked in the underground garage of his apartment building.

The only problem in using the bike was the cancerous pollution, so he not only had to strap on a helmet and gloves but also a mask, black with yellow flames, just like a race enthusiast. It was an unlikely flash of personality considering his shy character but since it had the additional benefit of covering his skin affliction, he allowed his ego to enjoy this minor touch of flair.

10

That day, tensions ran high.

DEAN

"Cai just arrived," said the aide. "Says he needs to speak with you, in person and in private."

Dean glanced at his watch, figuring there was just no way Cai could have already found and spoken to the protest organizers. Yet this was a man Dean trusted, so he gave his assent, then waited until the former Agency analyst was facing him across the desk with the office door firmly closed.

"So?" he said simply.

"It's Xia," replied Cai.

Dean looked at him steadily. This seemed to match existing reports but it was nowhere near enough for a confirmation. "How do you know?"

"How do I know it's him? Or how do I know he's the only one it *could* be?" Cai had polished his English to a remarkable extent during his time here at the embassy.

"Both."

"The first is easy. It was his helicopter, his own personal transport."

"And how do you know that?"

Cai seemed insulted. "European model? Northern command markings? Give me some credit."

"All right, your second point. Why do you say he's the only one it could be?"

"My father knows him."

Dean had been fully briefed on Cai's background, including the estranged parental situation. It was all in the file. "Did they ever meet?"

"Once, in secret. Since then, they've always kept in touch."

"Okay, that's interesting but it doesn't answer the question."

"It does if you read into it. Xia wants Taiwan, always has. Wants to be remembered as the man who unified the nation, sees it as his great legacy. And my father wants the same on the other side. When they join hands, they become the bridge."

"Poetic."

"Thank you."

"Problem is, your father's not in power."

"No, but if Xia has enough juice over here, he can help get my father elected."

"How?"

"Are you kidding me? You know perfectly well how. Xia will apply all his resources to Taiwan. Manipulation, intimidation, whatever he has to do. Look what he did to the Russians up there in Harbin."

"I thought that was just an urban myth."

"No, it happened."

"Well, even if it did, you can't seriously compare that to this."

"Of course not. But I'm not making an analogy, I'm assessing a personality."

Again, Dean gazed across the desk at the man in front of him, this time for a longer period. "Okay, let's say for the sake of argument it *is* Xia. Wouldn't he just have his hands full with the same problems they've got now?"

"Maybe, maybe not."

"What's that supposed to mean?"

"He could just focus on what he wants and hand all other issues over to somebody else."

"Like who, for example?"

"One guess might be Shui."

"Shui? Really? He has to be over ninety by now."

"That's the point. He's too old to be a threat to Xia but old enough to be respected. Who better? He'd be the perfect foil."

"Shui's no leader."

"You're right, he's a follower. But that just means he hasn't upset anyone. He's a Party loyalist, goes all the way back to Mao. Any ideology you want, Shui's your man. Even wants to fix the environment or so they say, which would make him popular with those kids out there."

"You really think he's capable?"

"He doesn't have to be. Shui uses the general to enforce his demands. Xia uses the old man as political cover for the fact that he's military. It's perfect, the *yin* and the *yang*."

Dean disliked it when they brought out the clichés, all that eastern philosophy crap as if he were some kind of novice. But he didn't comment. He just opened a drawer, took out a small cloth and began to polish his glasses, a way to stall while he tried to digest the information he was being fed.

"This Xia," he said eventually. "Does he have any opposition in the ranks?"

"You mean is it unanimous? I seriously doubt it," said Cai. Then he added: "On the other hand, there's no denying he's widely admired across all divisions. And I'm sure *he* believes he's got the support, otherwise he wouldn't be doing it."

"Fair enough. And the militia?"

"Doesn't matter. If they follow him, fine. If they don't, there's not much they can do."

Dean thought about that before deciding it was yet another justified assessment. "How about the Guoanbu?" he asked. This was the common acronym for the Guojia Anquan Bu, the Ministry of State Security, the powerful, ubiquitous department which controlled all national aspects of intelligence, counterintelligence and undercover activity. "Where do you think *they* stand?"

Cai smiled briefly in recognition. When he worked upstairs at the Agency, he and his colleagues tended to regard the Guoanbu as their overarching nemesis and this, for him, was the real question.

"Who knows what goes through their heads at any given time?" he said quietly. "One thing I do know is that they have zero allegiance to anyone or anything. Whatever they decide, however they choose to respond, I guarantee it will only be in their own best interest."

"You think they'll play one side against the other?"

"Not necessarily, at least not in any active way. But they'll certainly be assessing the possibilities."

"Nice to be a fly on the wall over there right now," Dean said, almost to himself. "Okay, anything else you can add?"

"Not much. Just thought it was worth a chat."

"Well, thanks, appreciate you coming in. Oh, wait, one last thing," said Dean. "Know anything about an American trapped in there?"

"Where? Inside? I've heard nothing about that. Who is he?"

"Not clear yet. You think he's at risk?"

"I doubt it, not directly," said Cai. "But a lot of men with a lot of guns? You never know what can happen." Then he got up and strolled out of Dean's office in that deceptively casual way of his, heading off to who-knows-where.

ANDERS

The auditorium was becoming restless. The delegates had been through various stages of trauma, from shock to denial to fear, but now they were beginning to summon the strength to object. Despite the continued presence of several dozen armed troops, the hubbub was becoming louder and a few were on their feet, especially those up on the stage, who undoubtedly felt the need to demonstrate some kind of leadership.

If something didn't happen soon, Anders sensed they might just generate the will to resist. There were ten thousand in here and if they decided to take action en masse, it would leave the officers in command little choice but to retreat or to use physical force, perhaps even to fire. Although he had little knowledge of Chinese military structure, this squad didn't appear to be experienced military police with training in riot control. Instead, they appeared to be more of a raw frontline unit and if so, their primary instinct would be to react with whatever means they had available. In such a scenario, this could become a bloodbath.

Just when the noise seemed to be reaching crescendo level, several senior officers entered from the wings and strode out on stage. One in particular, a general, seemed to have more gravitas and it was he who stood at the rostrum, holding up his hand to demand silence. As a result, the audience settled a little, more from curiosity than from calm.

Up to this moment, the two men next to Anders had been among the most quiet and patient: Zhao because that was his nature; and more unexpectedly, Huang, who seemed to be biding his time as if assessing the situation. At last, it was the latter who spoke, muttering to himself as much as to his colleagues.

"What's he saying?" Anders asked Zhao.

"Mr. Huang is saying that he recognizes the general."

"The one at the podium? Who is he?"

There was some whispering between Zhao and Huang before the interpreter turned back to Anders.

"Mr. Huang says that he saw him once make a speech in Fujian province. The general's name is Xia."

"Is he sure?"

"Yes, Mr. Huang says the speech was about Taiwan, which as you know, is just off the coast of Fujian. There are historic ties between the two."

Even before Zhao had finished his explanation, Xia had begun to speak, aided by a thick wad of notes on the podium in front of him. From the formal introduction, it seemed like it was going to be a lengthy speech—obviously some kind of rationale for this action, perhaps even a manifesto—and while Anders was intensely interested in what the general had to say, he also felt the strong need to get this initial information to the outside world. As the sole American present, he believed he had an obligation.

ZHAO 赵

Once again, Zhao became apprehensive when he noticed Anders slip the secret phone out of his pocket. Most, if not all, of the others had been confiscated by the occupying force which now patrolled the aisles, threatening and intimidating with their assault rifles at the ready.

For his part, Zhao couldn't believe they would dare open fire in this crowded auditorium with so many senior party members present but he'd survived the Tiananmen massacre and he didn't wish to take any chances. To discourage his client, Zhao therefore placed a hand on the American's arm, hoping it would be enough of a signal but Anders turned away sharply to break free—and it was this movement that the passing officer noticed.

From the insignia, he appeared to be mid-level, maybe a lieutenant, and he immediately ordered a nearby corporal to seize both the phone and the man using it, pointing out the highly visible Caucasian for all to see. Immediately, the young NCO obeyed by sidling through the row of delegates with neither tact nor diplomacy.

However, before he could reach Anders, it was Zhao who got to his feet. Since he felt at least partially responsible for causing the problem, he wished to talk to the young serviceman, to reason with both him and the officer, but he wasn't given the chance. When he refused to obey a sharp command to sit down, he was jabbed firmly in the chest with the rifle stock, doubling him over in pain before the weapon struck him again on the upswing, this time finding the cheek bone, splitting the skin and causing his blood to flow.

With the lieutenant still issuing commands, the corporal took the wounded Zhao roughly by the arm and dragged him out, with Anders following along, remonstrating as best he could. It had zero effect on the lieutenant, who grabbed the extra phone from the foreigner and smashed it under his boot. Then he demanded the American's passport, too, before leading them both toward the exit. In the rear was the corporal, alternately prodding his two victims with the gun muzzle in order to hurry them along.

At the doorway, Zhao managed to glance back to where Huang was still seated, having done nothing at all to help, his instinct for self-preservation obviously making sure that he remained, like the crows to which he aspired, well above this particular fray.

XIA 夏

From where he stood, the general could just about make out some minor problem in the back of the hall, a pair of troublemakers being hauled away, but he refused to let that faze him at such a critical stage.

This was the moment he felt it would all come together, recognition or rejection, success or failure. He was conscious of it and he had to clear his throat several times, perhaps due to apprehension or simply to rid himself of the bad air from outside. He wished he'd thought to pour himself a glass of water but it was too late now. What he was doing was too crucial.

In this, his maiden speech, he would have to soothe anxieties in order to avert any primary instinct for negative reaction. He would need to tell these representatives, the most important in the country, that this was not a revolution but simply an *evolution*; that the Party he admired and loved would remain firmly in power as it had since the People's Republic was founded; that the military had no wish to seize control, nor to change its mandate; that only the Standing Committee would be replaced because they'd failed in their responsibilities; that their blows against corruption were a sham for propaganda purposes only; that their agreements on the environment were too far into the future to affect anything, while hundreds of thousands of hardworking countrymen were today suffering and dying from the lax regulations; that the youth out in the square, their own children, were being alienated.

And it was for these reasons that he was nominating a true Party loyalist to be temporary chairman of the committee until new appointments could be announced, a stalwart whose credentials were impeccable, whose respect was universal—and only then, only after these inspiring words, would he reveal the name of Shui, which he believed would go a long way to ease the tensions.

In fact, it was Shui who'd coached him when writing this speech. Usually when military men spoke, Shui had told him, what came out of their mouths was the harsh and ugly truth, which made them unpopular with everyone except their own troops. Experienced politicians, on the other hand, knew how to paint a finer picture, at once more hopeful and aspirational, and if Xia wanted to haul these delegates aboard, he would not only have to color his vision in beautiful tones but also provide a thick coat of varnish to reassure them. That was the price to be paid, the old man had insisted, in order to realize a vision.

Besides, redemption could always be achieved through success. That was the one ingredient that turned politicians—or generals for that matter—into statesmen, and while Taiwan might be an emotional subject for the Chinese people, there was a limit to how much they'd tolerate in order to achieve that aim. Only when the island was finally back in the fold as an integral part of the nation would the man who made it possible be recognized as the people's hero.

Until that time, don't even mention Taiwan, Shui had advised, no matter how justified. His advice was to hide it, sequester it, bury it under a general promise of addressing ordinary daily grievances. Use that as your rationale and stay away from any mention of offshore expansion. Accession to power by military force would always be controversial, Shui had warned him, so apply the varnish so thick that it's opaque.

This was therefore a long speech that Xia had prepared, full of glowing tributes, classic quotations and general optimism, and he waded through it with as much enthusiasm as he could muster. And even as he was still talking, an information package containing the entire text, a selection of key points plus official portraits of himself and Shui, was being presented outside to the only member of the media who really mattered, the senior representative of the Xinhua news agency. It would now be that man's task to distribute it throughout the country and to the rest of the world.

QIAN 钱

The general's statement became the first major headline as the internet flickered back to life on Qian's phone. While the content was astonishing—a change of government right here in front of him—he wasn't at all surprised at its method of delivery. This was how the media was managed because it was purely at the service of the Party, a state of affairs which had always caused so much exasperation to the recently deceased Chen.

The problem was that as the information trickled out, it was beginning to divide the crowd into the majority, who desperately wanted to believe the ideals as stated, and the more wary, who were of the opinion that this was just another ruse, that it couldn't be taken at face value, that it was simply a means of obscuring a grab for power.

As for the small organizing group around Qian, they too were becoming polarized, and he was a little surprised to see that the arguments on each side were being led respectively by the couple who normally held similar opinions, Sun and Feng. While the former, with his naturally positive attitude, was more prepared to believe, it was the latter with all her courtroom acumen who was the more cynical.

"What if I'm right?" Sun was insisting. "What if this really is the beginning of reform?"

"It's not," Feng replied, but her reflex answer was far too definitive for Sun.

"You don't know that for sure. Shouldn't we wait and see, give them the benefit of the doubt?"

"What benefit? Xia's a hardliner, always was. He built his career on it."

"Not Shui, though. He's been one of the strongest supporters of the current progress."

"What progress?"

"Well, tougher penalties for polluters for one thing."

"That's all just for show," argued Feng.

"So you say but what if it's not? What if he's been trying hard and failing because he's old and has no real power left? Maybe he wants to push it more aggressively and thinks that being allied with the army is the only way."

"I can't believe you're defending him."

"And you're a defense lawyer, so I can't believe you're *not*," replied Sun. Then he looked around at each of the group in turn. "Am I the only one?" he asked, his tone rising. "Isn't this exactly what we want? Isn't this why we're all out here getting lung cancer? We want something done about the environment and this is what Shui represents. What's wrong with that?"

"I know you want to believe him," said Feng with equal vigor. "So do I. So do we all. They're nice words but how often have we heard such nice words?" At this, she paused as if realizing that she just wasn't getting through to Sun, or to any of them, and wasn't sure how else to cope, so she turned to Qian who'd been listening to the debate along with everyone else. "What do *you* think?"

"What I think," he said, "is that we should all keep our voices down."

Personally, he could understand Sun's point of view as much as Feng's but his own greatest concern was not whether to believe the stated intentions but whether the arguments could ever be resolved. To him, it was by no means certain that this new cabal of Xia and Shui would find it that easy to seize complete control of the country or even of the Party. There were a great many who owed their entire careers to the current leadership and he wasn't sure they'd be willing to surrender all of that so readily.

SHUI 水

Within an hour, the man whose position within the hierarchy had declined with age to the level of director of sports administration had suddenly been redeemed, elevated to a higher status than he'd ever achieved.

He was now chairman elect of the Standing Committee, the supreme guiding authority of the world's most populous nation, and he hadn't even left his small office overlooking Tiananmen. The hope had been to move so rapidly that the transfer of power became a fait accompli before the reactionary forces could rally and so far, reports were suggesting that this was indeed the situation.

As for the state media, their response was more neutral, which was really to be expected since they no longer knew where their loyalties lay. A few had decided to throw their support behind the coup, saying it was a noble move and gambling that the new situation would hold. Others, including many of the major organs, were still keeping their options open. Only one bold editor in Shanghai had come out strongly against the action and had even begun calling Xia and Shui the "Gang of Two," a derogatory phrase recalling the period immediately after Mao's death when his widow and three others, together known as the "Gang of Four," had tried to assume power before being deposed and branded as traitors.

More interesting for Shui, however, was that so far, foreign commentary also seemed to be muted, especially the western networks, which were announcing through a series of newsflash bulletins that some kind of regime crisis was in the process of taking place, with their analysts and pundits frantically trying to assess the state of affairs without actually taking sides. While no one was recognizing this change as a military putsch or even an outright coup d'état, there was no outright rejection of such a premise either, which seemed to Shui to demonstrate how little faith anyone had in the current leadership.

At a certain point, while the general was still only part way through his speech, Yu came in to suggest that since it was all proceeding very much as planned, they should perhaps transfer over to the auditorium.

Shui was a circumspect man, always had been, and he'd been deliberately biding his time up here within the confines of his office but at this juncture, he found himself in agreement that a little more optimism was permissible.

HUANG 黃

Although he'd been disturbed at the fate of the American and his interpreter, Huang believed that there were greater stakes at issue and that it would be more prudent to remain equitable for the time being. He'd therefore determined that he should just sit and listen in order to assess more completely what impact today's events might have on himself and on his own sizeable empire.

The problem was that Xia's speech was droning on for far too long. These pompous elaborations, so common within the auspices of the National Congress, were tiresome in the extreme to a plain-spoken man like Huang. And all of it had been said so many times before: less corruption, less pollution, more social harmony, more national pride, etcetera.

In fact, the only time Huang really began to wake up was toward the end when the name of his old pal Shui was introduced. Now this was news, a huge surprise about which Huang had received no warning at all, not even a hint. The old man must have been planning this for months but there'd been no word, no leak, nothing at all to suggest what might be happening.

Yet this was quickly becoming the all-important issue for Huang. How much actual change would there be? He was well used to reading between the lines of propaganda to detect the underlying trends but this was considerably more difficult.

In the end, he figured that it could all be summarized by just two alternative scenarios.

Either Xia could be taken at his word that there would be a crackdown on the current system, or he was lying like all the rest of them and everything would continue as before. If the latter, then it meant that this entire coup was a wonderful bargain as far as Huang was concerned, because with the mere tripling of his contribution to Shui, he now had instant access to the Party's supreme authority. But if the former, then he was starting to appreciate that he'd have to recalculate his entire operation.

It wouldn't necessarily be threatening from a financial point of view, since most of his liquid assets had already been funneled away to Europe and elsewhere, but if they began prosecutions, he was thinking he'd do well to start planning for himself and his family to follow their money abroad. And if so, they should probably leave sooner rather than later because once the military had him behind bars, he might never again see the light of day.

Such existential questions had been churning around inside Huang's brain for much of the speech until his thoughts were interrupted by the most dramatic climax of all. The general stretched out his arm, pointed his finger and in his most stentorian voice, ordered the arrest of all seven current members of the Standing Committee.

By that stage, the room had been reduced to a hush and like Huang, the delegates all just watched, some with mouths open, as their revered leaders got to their feet and filed out like low-class criminals on their way to the prison wagon. It was humiliating in the extreme but then, Huang figured, that was the desired effect, to have them pass from mythic preeminence to seedy impotence in order to prove just how fleeting was their true authority.

Only after that did Xia finally get around to introducing the man who was already in the wings, the old man whom Huang knew well. To applause and to a certain amount of relief from the delegates at this familiar face, Shui mounted the podium and stood for a while, just surveying his audience in order to absorb what was undoubtedly a sweet moment for him.

Once he began to speak, his tone was not as confident as the general's but the audience seemed to appreciate it more. Respect seemed to have replaced conjecture as the overall mood, Huang was thinking, which augured favorably if this dangerous adventure was to succeed. It was a dual approach: the hard line of Xia and the mild tones of Shui, the disciplined authority and the venerated elder. As a strategy, it had been well considered.

ANDERS

After being forcibly removed from the auditorium, Anders had been separated from his interpreter and prodded into a cargo elevator for the short descent to the basement.

Here, he was marched along an empty corridor and pushed into a dimly lit room, with the door locked behind him. Apparently, this would be his makeshift cell. Essentially it was just a concrete storage space lined with a maze of pipes and containing only a pile of sealed drums plus several stacks of plastic chairs. The worst aspect was the smell, a mix of harsh cleaning fluids and whatever soy-drenched concoction the janitorial crew had consumed for lunch.

Outraged at such treatment, Anders struggled to control both his temper and his thought process. He knew he'd been impulsive, that he'd been stupid to think he could act like a second-rate secret agent, sending out text messages as if this were some crass Hollywood production. He also felt sick about Zhao, at the way they'd struck him simply for trying to defend his client. But beyond all of that was the nagging realization that they might now be planning some sort of show trial at which he'd be paraded in front of the cameras, accused of espionage and charged accordingly.

Of course, in such a circumstance, the embassy would make its inevitable demands and the State Department would issue a formal complaint to the new leadership, all of which would be highly appropriate, except that it would probably make no difference. He would still be found guilty and sentenced to—what? Prison time? Hard labor? Would the Agency then have to find some jailed Chinese hacker they could exchange for him, like one of those old Cold War spy swaps? Failing that, how far would the White House go to obtain his release? Would they put half a trillion in trade on the line? Of that, he was less certain.

Far more likely, he thought, he'd be left to his own fate, nothing more than collateral damage on the way to reestablishing some sort of superpower stability.

ZHAO 赵

The wound on his face was stinging and the pain in his rib cage was excruciating but to Zhao these were no more than warning signals within his concussive delirium that there might be worse to come.

The ox had stood his ground against the crows but now that he was down, they were all over him, hauling him along passageways and through doorways as if in slow motion. He saw lights flashing and could taste the grit in the outside air but he was hardly aware of any of it because the ominous wings were all around him, darkening the yellow sky and obscuring his vision.

He winced as somebody dabbed his cheek, talked to him, asked him questions, yet all he could hear was the raucous noise of the huge birds as they wheeled and floated, eager to attack their downed prey, and he sensed that soon, very soon now, they would be feeding voraciously on his flesh, their beaks the color of oxblood as they tore him apart.

ANDERS

For what seemed like hours, Anders sat on one of the plastic chairs, eyes half-closed and head in his hands, trying to analyze the likelihood of his fate, with each possibility only serving to drain his reserves further and accentuate the headache that the odor was causing. The confident, can-do attitude that had driven him to the global heights of commerce was starting to fail him and he knew he shouldn't allow it.

Yet despite all his years of travel, this was the first time he'd ever been in such a situation. He'd been told about it endlessly by his security consultants, briefed on what he should be thinking, feeling, doing, in order to come to terms with it but he was still fighting with himself, trying not to assume the worst.

Then all at once, a new opportunity presented itself. The door was thrust open and in strode General Xia himself, accompanied by several of his officers. One of them, the lieutenant who had originally ordered the arrest, handed the general the seized passport and Xia rapidly leafed through the pages.

"Your name is Anders?" he said in halting but adequate English.

Anders was already on his feet, at last ready to exhibit some defiance. This wasn't his mind playing its deceitful tricks. This confrontation was real, something he could handle, and he felt the adrenaline begin to flow, the American blood coursing through his veins.

"Yes, my name is Anders," he replied firmly. "I'm a US citizen and I demand that you release me immediately."

The general remained expressionless. "You are here why?"

"I was invited by Director Shui."

A slow reaction. "You know Shui?"

Anders wanted to impress with both his status and his standing but he held himself in check. Lying at this stage would be stupid. "Shui personally invited a man called Huang," he explained, "and it was Huang who invited me."

Xia looked at him steadily. "Okay, I understand."

"Understand? Understand what?"

"This is a . . ." The general paused, searching for the word. "A mistake," he said, pleased with himself for finding it.

Anders was in no mood to congratulate him. "A mistake?" he repeated loudly. "You throw me in here, you hurt my interpreter . . ."

"Who?"

"My interpreter, Zhao."

Here, the lieutenant whispered something before the general answered. "Ah, your man. Yes, he is okay, no problem."

Anders wanted more information. He needed to know details, about Zhao's injuries and if they were being treated, but before he could press further, Xia was already changing the subject.

"You have contact with your people?"

"My people?"

"Yes, yes, your people, your government. You have contact?"

There was a hesitation until Anders remembered his pal Hoyle in Berlin. "In a way . . . through a friend."

"Ah, a friend, yes, good. Please tell your government friend we have only warm hearts for the United States. We wish only for good relations."

"You can tell the United States yourself. I'm sure they're anxious to hear from you."

Xia looked as if he didn't really follow, as if that was too much for him to translate, but it didn't seem to matter. He had his own agenda. "Two ways to talk," he continued, holding up a couple of thick fingers. They were the fingers of a soldier, yet the nails were perfectly manicured. "Direct way and friend way. You are friend way, okay?"

He reached out his hand and Anders just looked at it for far too long. But then he took it anyway and allowed the single shake as if it were an international peace agreement.

"Am I free to go?"

The general gave him back the passport. "Free, yes."

"And Zhao? My interpreter?"

The general was dismissive, as if it were an issue of no consequence. "Yes, yes." Then he turned stiffly and left, full of his own arrogance, followed by most of his retinue. Only the lieutenant was left standing by the door of this makeshift cell, holding it open.

Anders didn't delay. He was more than glad to be out of confinement, to be rid of that pungent stench, as he walked alongside the officer toward the same cargo elevator. This time there was no force applied, no rifle in the back, just a polite ride to the surface.

Once outside, Anders cleared his lungs with a major bout of coughing, then scanned the large semi-circle of people but there was nobody he recognized—neither Zhao, who he hoped was at some clinic by now, nor Huang, who he figured might still be inside. Instead, all he saw in the immediate vicinity was the heavy security, the line of tanks and the pressing media, with the same journalist stepping forward.

"Mr. Anders," she called over. "Ren from *China Daily*."

"Yes, I remember."

"Please, a word. How are you feeling?"

He certainly had no wish to speak to her but answered anyway. "I'm fine."

"May I have your reaction to these events?"

"I have no comment at this time."

He tried to move away but she was insistent.

"Mr. Anders, will you be talking to your government?"

"I have no comment."

"Are you going back to America now?"

He was tired of repeating the same words, so he just held up his palm and tried a faint smile to imply that he had nothing against either the media or the lady herself but that his stance was firm.

Yet it also occurred to him that at this precise moment he had no way of going anywhere at all, not even to the hotel. He'd arrived with the others in the limousine, which had immediately returned to its home base, and he certainly didn't feel like hiking all the way back alone. It was ridiculous after all he'd been through but the only option was to head over to Chang An and find a taxi, if any were still running.

However, just as he advanced past the media trucks and beyond the security barrier, a black-garbed figure on a Japanese bike came to a stop in front of him.

"Get on," said the man in English. He had just the hint of an accent.

Anders looked at the man, at the face mask with the flames, and wasn't too eager to let himself be taken captive yet again. "No thanks."

"You know the name Hoyle?"

"What? Who the hell are you?"

"Just get on."

Anders thought about it, still unsure whether to risk a lift with this anonymous individual, but the mention of his friend helped convince him. Besides, it wasn't like he was being tossed into the back of a van. This was just a bike and in theory he could simply slide off whenever he wished.

"Where are we going?" he asked as he climbed aboard. But there was no answer, just an impatient revving of the machine.

DEAN

The visitor looked sallow and still a little frazzled, so Dean felt duty-bound to offer some empathy.

"Must have been some ordeal," he said, welcoming the man into his office with as much bonhomie as he could muster.

"Just glad to be out of there," Anders replied.

"Well, we're all glad you made it safely." Dean graciously indicated the small spread on the table, a plate of sandwiches and some chips in a bowl. "Please, help yourself. I took the liberty of ordering from the cafeteria. We can grab something more substantial later." He lifted a thermos. "Coffee? Water? Or something stronger?"

"Coffee's fine, thanks."

Dean poured for the two of them, then brought his chair around the desk so the chat could be a little more informal. "So, Mr. Anders, talk to me."

"It was Xia."

"Yes, that much we know."

"No, I mean he came to see me."

"Personally?"

Anders took a mouthful and washed it down with the hot beverage before he could respond. "They shut me in the basement, over two hours with a guard on the door. Disgusting place. Then suddenly, what do you know? In walks Xia himself with a bunch of subordinates. Wanted to apologize, show me how friendly he is."

"Doesn't *sound* too friendly."

"Zhao got it worse."

"That would be your interpreter."

"You spoke to him?"

"He called us a few minutes ago."

"He did? How is he?"

"Some bruising, abrasions, nothing too serious."

"They released him?"

"Apparently."

"Good ol' Zhao. Stood up to them like a hero, only one in the whole place."

"Did you get the impression there was support for the coup?"

"From the delegates? I don't know. They just seemed kind of stunned. Even Huang couldn't say much, rare for him."

"Huang?"

"Sportswear. Big money. Friend of Shui, by the way. That's how he organized it for us."

"Us? You mean you and Zhao?"

"Also my vice president—which reminds me, I haven't heard from her since this morning."

"She's American?"

"Yes. Well, no. What I mean is she's a Canadian citizen based in Hong Kong. Her flight was diverted to Tianjin but she didn't show up. I hope she's okay."

"Well, we can look into that for you."

"Do you think . . . No, why would they arrest her? It makes no sense. None of this makes any sense. I don't know why they'd . . . unless . . ."

Anders was munching on his sandwich, drinking his coffee and attempting to speak all at the same time. His mind was obviously racing and Dean could detect signs of post-traumatic stress. He'd seen it before in an earlier life, at the mission in Kabul where he was stationed for a brief period after the Taliban had been ousted.

"Mr. Anders, try to relax. You're here now and you're safe. As I said, we'll make inquiries about your employee but meanwhile, why don't you tell me exactly what happened? From the top, all right? Every detail you can remember."

11

That day, events moved rapidly.

CAI 蔡

In a hyper-modern coffee shop close to the embassy district in Chaoyang, Cai was adding sugar to his cappuccino, indulging in his own ritual of stirring it methodically into the creamy froth. Directly opposite him was Wang, the man who once had the job of following Cai around the city on behalf of the Guoanbu, the overarching state security service which maintained a rote surveillance on anyone with whom they had a modicum of suspicion.

Since Cai was just an analyst, it was hardly a high-profile assignment for Wang, nor was it especially challenging since his target's skin discoloration made him more than evident on any street. However, that little game was all in the past, back when Cai was still on the CIA payroll. These days, he was enjoying a more lucrative position in private security and Wang, too, had moved up in the world, having ascended with equal rapidity thanks mainly to the rise in prominence of his department head. That's how things were done in the nation's bureaucracy. When a top man climbed the ladder, so did his key underlings and of these, Wang had been the prime recipient of his superior's good fortune.

Now, as a pair of seasoned professionals, still in the same covert business but no longer in direct confrontation, Cai and Wang met occasionally to gossip, to catch up and to exchange views, especially if there was anything special to discuss—and today, there happened to be a great deal.

They'd chosen a table in the corner away from anyone but still, Wang glanced around before speaking as a matter of habit.

"And what do your friends at the Agency think of all this nonsense?"

"Is that your official position?" said Cai. "That it's nonsense?"

"No, that's my own, until proven otherwise. But you're avoiding my question."

"That's because I didn't meet with the Agency."

"Who then? Your *good buddy* Dean?"

Wang chose to use the American phraseology as part parody, part insult, but the Guoanbu knew well enough that Cai's ongoing association with the embassy was merely networking, just some routine freelance work, so the accusation was no more than a friendly taunt.

Cai chose to reply in kind. "I'm just a simple man with a simple philosophy," he said. "I work for whoever pays me the most. That way I don't have to worry about something as trivial as a military coup."

This was how it was between the two of them, their exchanges never failing to include a measure of sarcasm and disparagement. In this case, Wang offered the slightest of grins, then put his cup down and became serious, as if he needed to end the small talk.

"Tell me what we're doing here."

Cai waited for an attractive waitress to pass by on her way to the kitchen. Once she was out of earshot, he looked back across the table. "I'm wondering if you're going to act."

"Is this coming from you or from Dean?"

"Does it matter?"

"Yes, it does."

In his call to set up this meeting, Cai had hinted that he was delivering a message from the embassy without being overly specific. "If I'd told you this was my own initiative, would you have come?"

"Probably not."

"So there you are."

Wang sighed, as if this was turning out to be nothing but a waste of his time on such a critical day. "All right, so I'm here now. Say what you have to say. I'll do you the honor of listening."

Cai hesitated for several seconds, debating with himself how honest he should be, before finally coming to a decision. "I can't let him win," he said quietly.

"Who? Xia or Shui?"

"My father."

"Ah," said Wang, nodding his comprehension. He knew all about the stormy family ties because within his counterintelligence division, they made it their business to know everything about everybody. They had sufficient resources to keep files on over a billion citizens within the borders, as well as millions more beyond.

Cai sipped his coffee. "Are you?" he asked again.

"Are we what?"

"Going to act?"

"Act? How? What do you think we can do? You think we have a couple of armored divisions at our disposal? Maybe a stash of weaponized drones for black ops like your old friends at Langley?" At this point, Wang offered an even broader smirk. "Or maybe you think our analysts will get up from their keyboards and arm themselves with kitchen knives from the cafeteria?"

Wang seemed to enjoy his own humor but Cai was less appreciative.

"What I think is that you can do just about anything you want."

"Actually, that's not true. It just seems that way from the outside."

"Do you, or do you not, have people embedded in every regiment?"

"People, yes," said Wang. "But that's the problem. People are human and we can never be totally sure where their true loyalties lie." Then he added, "That's classified, by the way. Don't spread it around." He meant the last part as yet another joke but it was closer to reality than anyone in his ministry would ever dare acknowledge.

"My point is still valid," said Cai. "You could stop them if you wanted."

Again, Wang opened up that strange half-grin of his. "You really don't like your father very much, do you?"

Cai was also beginning to tire of the badinage. At any other time, he might have found it entertaining but today was different. "You don't have to go up against the army," he said quietly. "You just have to eliminate one man."

"Just like that."

"Why not? A bullet to the head and it's over."

"You mean a sniper from a mile away? In this visibility? You think we haven't thought of that?"

Cai just shrugged. "There are other methods."

"Really? You have a suggestion to offer?"

"Oh, I'm sure you have far more creative minds than mine back at the office. The only thing you have to do is keep it as simple as possible. The more people involved, the more risk you take. Just keep it simple."

For a few moments, Wang nodded cautiously, allowing the thought to sink in and take effect. "All right, let's suppose we did manage to conceive something like that. You really think all the rest of them will just fall into line?"

"Cut off a crow's head, the body dies."

There was no answer from Wang and the concept continued to hang in the air between them until Cai began to tire of the silence. That was when he threw down some yuan for the coffee, got to his feet and walked out, quietly and without drama, just the way he'd done with Dean at the embassy. He'd never been one to outstay his welcome.

WANG 王

The man from the Guojia Anquan Bu remained in his seat, his mind full of thoughts until his coffee was cold. He knew perfectly well that the ideological fight between Cai and his politician father had as much to do with ego and spite as it did with issues of China and Taiwan and he was annoyed that he'd been called out on such a false premise.

On a personal basis, he liked Cai but he'd told his superiors that this contact would be delivering a covert message on behalf of the Americans, which obviously wasn't the case. Nevertheless, he wasn't overly eager to get back to the ministry, because discussions had become so intense as to be almost manic. Although no one there would admit it, they'd been taken by surprise by the speed of developments and as their record proved, that was an extremely rare occurrence. Of course, there would be retributions based on either negligence or stupidity, neither of which had ever been tolerated, but that would happen later. Meanwhile, they were arguing the pros and cons of the current situation endlessly at every conceivable level.

The great Guoanbu had a formidable reputation, almost an omnipotence within the national context, but they'd never before been challenged by the army, nor by anyone as ruthlessly competent as Xia. They knew his capabilities and that was the reason for the current indecision.

For them, the real problem was that any change, either positive or negative, was unpredictable. This new junta and their supporters might be sympathetic to the Guoanbu but there was no way to be certain and that had caused them to consider multiple possibilities, some of which had indeed included the ultimate option of assassination.

Unfortunately, as Wang had admitted to Cai, the success of any such solution would be based entirely on the loyalty of those involved. The overriding question for any course of action had therefore become how to guarantee the desired result. If somebody, anybody, chose to denounce the attempt, it would fail, causing the ministry to make an immediate enemy of the new regime and be in a far worse predicament than if they'd done nothing and remained neutral.

As for Wang himself, he'd been merely on the fringes of those internal debates. At his level, he hadn't been asked for his ideas and even if he'd offered them, few would have taken notice. Yet being here, away from the ministry and its swirling centrifuge of doubt, his head had cleared a little and he was beginning to place the situation in a different framework.

The three words that kept echoing in his head had come from his dubious friend. Keep it simple, Cai had said, which had given rise to a whole new way of thinking, a revised set of parameters. His concern wasn't so much the assassination of the general or even the method of delivery—whether that be a bullet to the head or some other means—as much as the necessity of ensuring that such an operation was completely foolproof in order to avoid any chance of betrayal within the long chain of command.

This was the concept that Wang was still formulating even as he took out his phone and tapped in a time-based code to obtain a secure line. It might well be that nobody at the ministry would even listen to some intermediate calling from a coffee shop but that didn't mean he shouldn't try.

XIA 夏

While the elderly Shui continued to offer his reassurance to the delegates in the Great Auditorium, Xia had passed from the smelly basement of the building, where he'd met briefly with that foreigner, to the prime elegance of the Anhui reception room.

It was to these luxurious surroundings that his officers had escorted the seven recently dethroned members of the Standing Committee, who were now seated around in plush armchairs. Naturally, they were deeply resentful at having been so humiliated in front of their Party leadership colleagues but at the same time, they seemed relieved that they weren't facing an immediate firing squad, as they might initially have imagined.

Despite the fact that they'd been removed from the Party Congress at gunpoint, Xia had wanted them to feel that they were not prisoners but participants, that this was not an ultimatum but a negotiation, an honorable effort to reconcile differences in the interests of the nation as a whole, and he was now trying to restore as much of their dignity as possible with a welcome offer. He was now suggesting they share power.

After seating himself in front of the group and making sure they all had tea, he began slowly, taking pains to explain fully and earnestly what he had in mind.

The proposal in its most elementary form was that each of them could remain in place exactly as before, as long as they agreed to the diarchy of Shui, in a newly created position as executive chairman of the Standing Committee, plus Xia as supreme commander of the Central Military Commission. If these honored Party loyalists could bring themselves to accept such leadership and follow a revised strategy, their status would be secure, as would the entire governing structure. This wasn't a military dictatorship, he assured them, far from it. This was merely a transition, nothing more, as peaceful and harmonious as they would wish it to be.

Once again, Xia was following Shui's advice with this approach. It was essential not to make threats, the old man had insisted. If any of them raises an objection, he'd said, don't try to shout him down. Just tell whoever it might be that we invite all contributions, that all ideas are valuable. Tell him anything to calm the concern but do not, under any circumstances, threaten the consequences of dissent, at least not openly, not at this stage.

Fortunately, such advice wasn't necessary. These veteran party chiefs, all survivors of much political infighting, did not object at all. Instead, they just sipped their tea, probing politely in their attempt to ascertain as many specifics as possible, and in this way, the discussion went on far longer than Xia had anticipated. He looked at his watch on several occasions but in fact, he didn't mind. This particular session was perhaps the most vital aspect of all today's events and he didn't want to hurry it when just a few extra minutes might make all the difference. If he could persuade these seven to continue serving, if only in the short term, it would instantly legitimize his new leadership, justify the entire process and rationalize everything that needed to be done.

Yet if none of them acceded to such an appeal, if they chose to react as a contrarian bloc, Xia had a strategy for that, too. In the face of such outright negativity, he would approach each on a personal basis and only then, in isolation and seclusion, would the consequences be spelled out: the lavish benefits and incentives of power sharing contrasted with the most severe consequences for refusal. At that stage, the amiable request would turn into the clearest of threats and whether the penalties would mean asset seizure, physical deprivation, family arrest, or direct accusation of treason with its predetermined death sentence would depend entirely on each person's response.

EE 鄂

Perhaps the only person in all of Beijing who didn't mind the atmospheric conditions was Private First Class Ee of the locally-based Jian special forces unit and he was currently gazing with some nostalgia at these yellow skies while being flown across the city in an officially commandeered police helicopter.

The young man's family home was in Hohhot, capital of the Neimenggu Autonomous Region, known to the rest of the world as Inner Mongolia. Situated on the edge of the Gobi, this area's famous grasslands were being eroded at an ever-higher rate. Yet despite all the environmental problems, Ee loved the encroaching desert, still dreamed of the barren landscapes he'd come to know while growing up. Now, each spring when the sand and grit returned to Beijing, it was as if the weather were paying tribute to his own youthful heritage.

Like so many in his native territory, he was of mixed parentage and as a child, he couldn't get enough of the stories his parents told him. While his Khalkha Mongol mother wove fabulous tales of her ancestral emperor, Genghis Khan, his Han Chinese father read to him each night about the warrior monks of Shaolin and their prowess in martial arts.

Of course, such stories were fantasies, nothing more, myths that had been embellished beyond all historical recognition. But to a city boy they were inspirations that fired up his imagination, so when he was obliged to quit school at fifteen and enter the family's commercial pipefitting business, he became discouraged enough to leave home, not once but twice. And since some of his earliest memories were of accompanying his father out to project sites in the desert, this became the favored destination for his runaway adventures, each time hitching a ride out to the bare foothills of the Yinshan, the mountain range bordering the Gobi, to seek his freedom in the expansive wilderness.

On the first occasion, he meandered alone for a week, plagued by the daytime heat and the long, cold nights, until he heard the bleating of goats and staggered dazed and malnourished into a rural homestead. On the next escape, he made sure to carry enough food but then took a bad fall from a rocky outcrop and would have bled to death if a mining engineer in his pickup hadn't been blessed with such keen eyes.

After almost losing their son, his parents came to realize that he'd never settle willingly into their enterprise but they couldn't come up with a suitable alternative career, until somebody in the family suggested the army, which seemed like a fine idea. Yet after signing up and living in a barracks for several months, that solution also frustrated the young man—until he learned about the mandate of the special forces, which from that time forward became his sole interest and ambition. While the rest of his platoon ridiculed such an obsession, nothing could dissuade him from applying again and again until his sheer persistence, coupled with his very evident enthusiasm, was duly rewarded.

Once he'd finally achieved the coveted transfer, he trained so rigorously that he passed every test on the first try, a record that few others had ever managed to achieve. As a result, even in such an elite outfit, he became a star recruit, both tough and conscientious, trusted enough that he could be assigned to active duty far earlier than most. So here he was, just a few years later, an experienced and proven member of the Jian unit, having been individually selected and fully endorsed for this mission by the embedded political liaison, a man whose loyalty to the Guoanbu ministry was unquestioned.

In fact, everything about this task had been arranged to minimize any chance of compromise and although Private First Class Ee had been individually briefed at the highest level by the Directorate of Field Operations, he was nevertheless denied access to either target identification or its political ramifications—no different from the sole operative who was now piloting him and his specialized equipment toward the central core in the craft they'd commandeered from the city's public security department.

Now, having circled around Tiananmen, they descended directly toward the ellipsoid concert hall, the modernistic venue on the other side of the Great Hall surrounded by broad acres of greenery and an artificial lake. As it happened, the thick atmosphere on this day was to their advantage, blocking most of the visibility from Chang An Avenue just to the north, but even if someone passing did happen to take an interest, it wouldn't matter because the brief touchdown within the parkland area would seem like nothing more than normal police activity.

YU 余

Of all the people who bore personal witness to the day's events, none had more anxiety about its audacity, or more wonderment in its achievement, than Shui's executive assistant, Yu. He was the one who had escorted the aging director over from his office and he was now the one who stood in the wings of the auditorium, waiting for the new chairman of the Standing Committee to wrap up his speech.

Never in all his long career had Yu imagined there could be a moment like this. For him it seemed to justify all the qualities he valued most: dedication, loyalty and effort, as well as the trust that his continued faith in such old-world virtues would eventually bring its own reward. But this was about more than just a work ethic. This was about pride of accomplishment, too, the apogee of achievement for an ordinary citizen such as himself. He was no great scholar, no princeling of the Party, no ruthless oligarch like that sportswear billionaire, Huang. He was just a man who'd tried to serve, to do whatever was asked of him with speed and efficiency, and above all to remain discrete, which meant keeping his own counsel at all times while revealing nothing at all about his function, even to his own family.

Over on stage, Shui was still acknowledging the applause, such as it was, and Yu could see that the old man was reasonably content with the reaction. Neither of them had been expecting an ovation, but both were satisfied that so many delegates would be pragmatic enough to accept the radical change, not as a direct challenge but as merely a revised version of reality.

This involved multiple promises by both Shui and before him, Xia, that on a daily basis everything would be the same and that the vast majority of Party members would keep their positions. Inevitably, there would be certain policy adjustments to manage but no more than in previous decades when the existing regime had handed over control to its successors and hopefully, this new coupling of civilian rule with army strength would prove to be a great deal more effective at enacting some long overdue reforms.

The way it was playing out, Yu was feeling ever more positive and as the old man came toward him, he shook the proffered hand with warmth and respect. "Congratulations," he said with genuine enthusiasm. "Excellent speech, very well done."

"We'll see," was the only reply. "Where's the general?"

Yu was surprised that Shui was not in more exuberant mood but such prudence, he assumed, was the nature of power. "We're due to meet him downstairs by the door."

"How did it go with the committee? Did you hear?"

"Not yet." Yu had been in constant touch with Xia's adjutant for purposes of coordination but all entry to the room known as the Anhui Hall had remained barred.

Shui grunted, which Yu took as permission to escort the new chairman out, past the military detail which was still guarding all exits from the auditorium and down to the lobby on the closed-off side of the building where the helicopter was waiting.

First though, they were obliged to strap on armored vests as the officers by the door were insisting. They'd be walking from the relative safety of the building across to where the aircraft was parked and nobody was willing to take any chances. The whole area was wide open and there was more than sufficient foliage between this building and the concert hall opposite to conceal an entire platoon of snipers. On balance, they didn't believe that such an assault was even a possibility in these adverse conditions but full precaution had been the general's order of the day and it was difficult to argue with that decision.

After a few more minutes, Xia arrived and he, too, was helped into a vest, signaling that their business here at the Great Hall of the People was now concluded and it was time to take the brief flight over to CCTV headquarters, where the new joint leaders were scheduled to make their primary broadcast to the nation.

The transport was ready, the rotor blades already turning, and all they had to do to reach it was traverse the thirty yards. For this, they were herded out in unceremonious manner by a twelve-man squad in battle gear, ranged into the classic diamond formation in order to cover the two principals and their aides from all sides. Due to age, the slowest among them was Shui, so the protection guard could only move at his geriatric pace and it all seemed to take far too long, with the thick air penetrating their lungs and the tension palpable at every step.

Somehow, it seemed that the closer they came, the more they were expecting something untoward to happen. Yet they managed to attain the shelter of the large craft without incident. Nobody had attacked, no sniper had fired, and the new dual leadership was quickly hustled aboard, closely followed by their aides, including Yu, who took his assigned place in the back and fastened his seatbelt with much relief.

It had been an astonishing day, nervous and enthralling in equal measure, and he was at last able to breathe a little easier as the machine lifted tentatively into the air, cleared the height of the Great Hall and then banked over the adjacent landscape.

That was when Yu glimpsed the bright flash from below, its diffused light breaking through the haze. From his perspective in the rear of the cabin, he might have been the only one to notice but since he had no technical expertise, he didn't think much of it. Such a flare could have been anything, perhaps just a work crew with a welding torch.

Then almost immediately, a slim, dark blur appeared in mid-air, weaving toward them, first this way, then that, but always accelerating. Once again, Yu became aware of it even before the pilot but had little time to warn anyone before the shoulder-launched, heat-seeking missile struck the craft and exploded into a flaming cataclysm of metal, glass and burning human flesh, with most of the debris falling as if in slow motion toward the shallow waters of the artificial lake below.

12 *That day, lives were changed.*

QIAN 钱

The sudden brilliance illuminated the sky above the Great Hall, accompanied by the resounding blast.

By this time, the young activists of Tiananmen had been augmented by an ever-growing mass of curious citizenry and all looked up as if in unison but even as itchy eyes searched the skies, the glow was fading and the echo subsiding. With the cause impossible to make out, they just turned to each other, the same wordless questions taking place all over the square.

After the initial reaction came the first stirrings of panic. Was that gunfire of some sort, maybe a tank shell? Nobody knew and nobody wanted to stay to find out. Even the uniformed personnel who were manning the concrete and wire barriers—army, militia, police—seemed to be stunned. While a few of the more effective officers were trying to reinstate discipline among their ranks, the civilians were already beginning to scatter, some falling over themselves in their haste to escape what they believed might well be the start of yet another carnage.

Qian, however, held firm. While Sun, Feng and others nearby were tempted to join the rush to leave, he refused to move, with Liang still clinging to him as she had for several hours.

"Wait, wait," he kept saying. "Look around. They're as surprised as we are. Nobody's shooting. This is something else."

"Like what?" said Sun.

"I'm not sure." But even as he said that, the thought came to him. "Maybe it was the helicopter," he suggested.

"Why would the army shoot down its own helicopter?"

Qian was still trying to piece it all together, trying to think quickly, but it was difficult. Too much was happening all around him. "This was a coup, right? So maybe there's some opposition." It was exactly what he'd originally feared.

"Which means what? Civil war?"

The question remained unanswered while Qian scanned the square. All around them, the crowd was thinning out, even as the various platoons were hastily assembling. Among them, Qian spotted his sometime friend, Sergeant Guan, along with the ever-dour Corporal Wei, who both looked back at him as if they were just as uncertain. Would they, too, be caught up in such a conflict?

Few present were of an age to recall the civil war of the late 1940s but all knew of it from their school textbooks, an ugly period of butchery between Chiang's so-called Nationalists and Mao's nascent Marxists. Each side had its adherents but after a decade of brutal occupation by the Japanese, it was Mao's socialist ideals which won over the bulk of the population. Under their tattered red banners, the ever-growing peasant army eventually gained enough of the countryside that Chiang and his forces were obliged to retreat to the offshore province of Taiwan where they remained, defeated but secure. Finally, in 1949, the mainland was triumphantly declared the People's Republic, with Mao and his communist cadre declaring their right to govern the new one-party state in perpetuity.

That wasn't the end of the suffering—indeed, for many it was just the beginning—but that former period of internecine conflict, known to all Chinese as the Glorious Revolutionary War, became firmly lodged in the popular mindset as a period of hardship and strife.

The question now in Qian's mind was whether anything similar could possibly happen again—and whether that mysterious explosion in the fading yellow sky was the first symbolic shot in some epic new struggle for control.

DEAN

Now that all systems were back up and functioning, the deputy chief of mission was once again watching his two screens simultaneously, the TV monitor and his personal computer. Already, solemn-faced studio anchors and their on-the-spot journalists were broadcasting updates, all conveyed with a mixture of urgency and tension.

"Do we have confirmation yet?" said Dean, catching the attention of an aide who happened to be passing by his open door.

"We think it was Xia's own transport."

"Yeah, me too, but I said confirmation."

"We're working on it."

For Dean, it had been a long day and it now looked like it was going to be an equally long evening, with all of Washington just waking up to this breaking drama due to the twelve-hour time difference. Very soon, he'd be inundated with requests for the reports, analyses and assessments he didn't yet have, all of which took time to pull together and review before they could be dispatched.

No sooner had the aide gone about his business than the ambassador herself arrived, sweeping into Dean's office like an empress.

"They're dead, both of them," she announced.

"What? Are we sure?"

"The ministry just called."

"Guoanbu?"

"No, Foreign Affairs. They want us to be in no doubt who's in charge. Said the 'Gang of Two' had perished and the Standing Committee had been freed."

"Is that for accreditation?"

"Not yet. They'll be putting out a formal statement soon."

"I guess Xia didn't have the support he thought he had."

"Apparently not," she said thoughtfully. "You think there'll be repercussions? Some kind of purge?"

Dean smiled but it was merely laconic, totally devoid of either warmth or humor. "Vast and bloody," he replied. That was when he heard new fragments from the TV broadcast and held up his hand to pause their conversation. "Wait, here it comes. They're talking about an accident at the Great Hall."

"An accident?" said the ambassador, not even trying to hide her incredulity.

Dean listened a while longer. His Chinese was by no means perfect, so he was obliged to furrow his brow and focus intently. "They're saying shigu, which usually means accident. What I'm not hearing is zhadan, the word for bomb or missile."

"You think that's official?"

"It's state media. They don't usually choose their own phraseology for stuff like that."

"So what does that mean? They're just going to flat-out deny the whole thing ever happened?"

"Wouldn't surprise me."

"The entire day erased, just like that." The ambassador shook her head. "Amazing," she said. "Absolutely amazing."

With that, she left as regally as she'd arrived, no doubt to get back on the phone with DC, leaving Dean to watch the ongoing bulletins. By this time, however, he was more preoccupied with his own thoughts.

The debate they'd now be having back at State, he believed, was whether to go along with the pretense or to come right out and tell the world that a military coup d'état had been attempted and overthrown within a matter of hours. The problem was the lack of hard evidence to support any such claim, since it was unlikely that anyone in the Politburo would ever go on record.

Eventually, of course, some of the thousands who'd witnessed the general's speech in the Great Hall would inevitably leak what really happened but Dean knew from experience that revealing the truth wouldn't be his own administration's main motivation. The factors that would determine their response would be more commercial than political. In other words, how much were they willing to conceal in order to avoid embarrassing this most essential trading partner?

HUANG 黄

Still trapped with all the delegates but without the benefit of cellular communications, Huang didn't yet know about events outside. They'd all heard something loud, which may or may not have been an explosion, but from deep within the building, it had been difficult to discern.

Then after a while, there was a new stirring of activity when no less than three senior generals strode across the stage, all with the same rank as Xia but none of whom Huang recognized.

It was the one in the lead who took the podium, grasping the microphone awkwardly as if it were too flimsy for his hand. But he didn't use it to address the Party delegates.

His words were directed toward the soldiers who were still stalking the aisles and guarding the exits, weapons in hand. There was no lengthy speech as before, no explanation at all. He just used his regular voice, clipped and precise, to inform the entire uniformed contingent that they were now relieved and that he was hereby commanding them to abort the mission without delay.

For several seconds, none of them knew what to make of this, especially the mid-level officers. It was as if their whole line of authority was being expropriated. They were aware that their original orders had come directly from Xia but it seemed as if those were now being revoked. Many glanced at each other for guidance but none had a ready solution. Ultimately, they had no real choice in the matter except to obey. A colonel was the first to move and, with some reluctance, began organizing his men to file out, an action that was slowly followed by all the rest, each still unsure where his own fidelity lay but none willing to face a court-martial.

Huang watched all of this from his seat at the back while he tried to figure out why this counterstrike might be occurring but he really didn't have enough information. Despite that, his brain continued to calculate the probabilities, his immediate thought being that if his old friend Shui had been removed from the equation, then there would be no requirement to increase the payments or, indeed, to pay anything at all.

Huang was still too cautious to make instant assumptions but he was slowly beginning to feel that his lifelong propensity for good fortune hadn't yet left him.

FENG 封

She was still there with Sun and the remainder of their small group as the yellow skies were fading to a dull shade of ocher.

Across the way, the soldiers who had so ominously rushed the Great Hall with weapons at the ready were now descending from that same stone edifice in a very different manner, not defeated as much as lethargic, as if it had all been a waste of time.

According to web reports, the leadership was now declaring that there'd been an emergency on this first day of Congress due to a threat of terrorist activity but that the people's security forces had responded with haste and proficiency to stabilize the situation. In certain other cities across the country, there had been similar incidents but all had been equally contained in a timely manner and there was no further danger to the public. The only casualties on the day, they said, were the occupants of a military transport helicopter which crashed by accident due to inclement weather with no survivors, plus an unrelated injury to a local bystander at Tiananmen, which also proved fatal. The government expressed regret for the tragic loss of life in both cases.

It was all nonsense and Feng knew it, just like everybody else in the square. No doubt future generations would whisper about this day, relating the events of Monday, March 19, 2012, as surreptitiously as those previous events of Sunday, June 4, 1989, because who would ever speak the truth out loud? Who would dare contradict the official version? Even the brave Chen, if he were still here, might have tempered his comments. Perhaps their aspirations had been overly optimistic but that didn't prevent the sense of disappointment, almost fatalism, that seemed to have enveloped them.

As for Feng herself, she'd remained more dubious than most, yet even she couldn't help thinking that maybe Sun was right, that an opportunity had indeed been lost.

They'd come here to protest the deadly toxicity and it seemed as if one old man, at least, had tried to address the problem, willing to acknowledge that too little was being done, that it was all taking too long. Had he merely been using nice phrases to seize control as she'd believed earlier, or was he being sincere, just another victim on the path to reform? Nobody knew, or would ever know, and it was this simple loss of hope which made it all so disheartening.

Yet Feng's legal training also allowed her to recognize the other side of the issue and she tried to console herself with a little reality.

When they arrived this morning, their greatest fear on viewing the excess security was that they might be caught in the same open slaughter as that previous generation but nothing of the sort had happened. Even when the police were threatening to use water cannon to disperse the crowd, it was the militia sergeant who had actually stood side by side right there with the intrepid Qian in order to prevent it.

To Feng, the irony of that single change was remarkable and surely a sign of progress—or at least that's what she was trying to convince herself. Despite the sad and unnecessary loss of their friend Chen, it was something she needed to believe and she took Sun's hand in hers as if to reassure herself that progress was still possible.

QIAN 钱

For an artist who'd sold his creative soul for a salary and an apartment, today had promised to be a time of redemption, a way to vanquish his own demons.

It was meant to be a grand gesture, made all the greater by the level of risk, a way to maintain his own idealism that a more civil society was possible if only the people wanted it badly enough, if only they insisted strongly enough.

This was still the People's Republic, he had reasoned, just as the building opposite was still the Great Hall of the People and those soldiers now leaving it still represented the People's Liberation Army. That was his rationale, the bravely simplistic underpinning of his most sincere beliefs, and it was for the people, as much as for himself, that he'd sincerely tried to make it happen. Throughout the day, he'd kept going, kept pushing, never surrendering to apathy even when it seemed more likely that tempers would erupt.

Now that it was over, though, he was asking himself what they'd accomplished. What was the net result if not a deeper depression for well-meaning activists, like the lawyer, Feng, or the architect, Sun, who'd regarded him since boyhood as something of a mentor? He felt he'd failed them and failed Liang, too, who was still holding on to him, still in anguish about Chen. All he could do was make some small amends by offering to escort her back to her abode and making sure she was all right—except she didn't want to go home, couldn't face the emptiness.

Liang was alone now in the city, without rights and without a roommate to share her troubles, so when Qian suggested in all innocence that she could come stay with him for a while, it was like a salvation. He had the space, he told her, and she could have her own room but even before he could complete the thought, she was nodding her acceptance and her gratitude. Her cheeks were still sore from the endless stream of tears but her bloodshot eyes became just a little brighter.

It meant that instead of helping thousands, possibly millions, Qian would find his peace on this day by helping just one and for now, that would have to suffice.

LIANG 梁

Her mind was empty, her spirit broken, and she'd become no more than a ghostly wraith. After all the years of financial struggle and moral compromise, of city life and village culture, the nervy willpower that had for so long held her together had at last given way.

All she knew was that somehow her wayward soul had attached itself to this tether who called himself Qian and she couldn't let go, either physically or psychologically, because there would be nothing left to prevent her from floating away, drifting as if by random and vanishing into the ether of oblivion, no more than a figment of her own imagination.

Her attachment to him was simply a lifeline and she continued to hold him as closely as possible, to feel his presence next to her as proof that she was still a part of reality.

CAI 蔡

As the heavy dusk descended, the final troop carriers began leaving the square and although many of the militia and police units remained on duty, there was little for them to do. Tiananmen was thinning out and after what happened today, Cai doubted that the crowds would be back tomorrow. The environmental protest was over, as indeed was the coup d'état.

He would never be sure about his contributions to this day, how much his few words had managed to breathe some fresh thinking into the mighty Guoanbu, but the results were there for those with sufficient insight. Not only had the course of events been changed but the lifelong ambitions of his imperious father over in Taipei had been placed on hold and that, for Cai, was no small accomplishment.

Despite all of that, he wasn't really in the mood to celebrate, because by zero-sum process, saving his own island for democracy also had the effect of maintaining the status quo here in Beijing and he wasn't at all sure that he wished to continue living in such a place. Human existence was just too short for such sacrifice, which meant that he was now faced with the decision of what he wanted to do with the rest of his days.

No doubt there would always be opportunities for a trained security professional on just about any continent, perhaps with the Americans, perhaps with somebody else. Yet while that might represent valid ambition for a true mercenary, Cai also recognized that it was a sad commentary for anyone with a conscience about how life should be.

ANDERS

For most of the people who'd been directly involved, the day was over but for the sole outsider, the only western eyewitness to these events, a modicum of guilt remained.

There'd been no need for his old friend, Zhao, to stand up for him like that. The man was an interpreter, not a bodyguard, and if he'd chosen to remain seated, that would have certainly been justified. But Anders had been headstrong, far too used to taking the lead and getting his own way, and now the personal shame continued to nag.

To be sure, a reward of money could in no way assuage what happened and in other circumstances might even appear tasteless. Nevertheless, it was the best idea Anders could devise and he therefore multiplied Zhao's usual daily fees by a factor of ten. He also offered to pay any medical expenses and to book him into the hotel, inviting him to rest up as long as he wished. Then, in addition to all of that, he promised something he should have offered years ago—a salaried retainer to be on permanent call for the company, which he knew would help provide a considerable degree of financial stability.

As for himself, he thought he would have been prepared for such a trauma, believed he'd been expertly trained by the security specialists back home, but when it came to it, he felt as if he'd failed the test and all he could do now was thank whichever guardian angels had been assigned the task of protecting idiot executives. He was well aware that it could have all ended a lot worse and he was psychologically exhausted after the experience.

The intense apprehension generated by what he thought might well be a death sentence had totally depleted his energy but on returning to the hotel, he'd found a message from the embassy waiting for him. In the flattest of consular prose, the night duty officer wished to advise him that they'd finally managed to locate his vice president in a Tianjin hospital, that she'd been involved in a vehicular incident, but that she was making progress and the prognosis was positive.

For the moment, Anders wasn't sure what to do. He was desperately fatigued, yet he also felt the urgent need to get over there, so he took a vibrantly hot shower, changed his clothes and once again called down to reserve the hotel car and driver.

EE 鄂

Even after he returned to base, the young man from Hohhot who loved the windswept desert still had no clue about what he'd managed to accomplish with that single missile fired from his shoulder. No one informed him that he'd just assassinated two of the most prominent public figures or that with his action he'd probably changed the entire course of the nation.

All that occurred was that his sergeant shook his hand, congratulated him on his success and ordered him placed in custody.

Then without explanation, Private First Class Ee of the Jian special forces unit, former star recruit, was escorted in handcuffs to the familiar training compound behind the barracks along with the operative who flew him on his mission. There they were blindfolded, forced to their knees and promptly dispatched by that same sergeant with a bullet to the side of each head, just two more deaths sanctioned by the eternal demand for harmony.

TSE 谢

She was heavily bandaged and still lightheaded from the painkillers they were pumping into her but she awoke when he walked in and was visibly pleased to see him.

"Hey boss," she said, her voice no more than a hoarse mumble as she felt him take her hand in his.

"I'm sorry, I didn't find out until late. How're you doing?"

"Raring to go," she said, attempting a smile.

He helped her to sit up, stuffing an extra pillow behind her back to make her as comfortable as possible. That's when she examined his face more intently, squinting at him through weak eyes.

"You look like hell," she said.

"Yeah, been that kind of a day."

"Did I miss anything?"

It was a perfectly straightforward question and she was a little disconcerted when his only reaction was to break into laughter, so much so that it even caught the attention of his driver who was just outside, waiting politely on a bench in the corridor.

"What?" she asked. "What did I say?"

By this time, Anders was almost choking on his own hysteria. For Tse, it was a strange sight, almost surreal for her to witness him in this state, and all she could do was lean back and wait for it to subside.

ZHAO 赵

As a professional interpreter, Zhao's career had allowed him the occasional privilege of staying in the same luxury accommodations as his clients but it was by no means a familiar occurrence. That's why, early the following morning, he found it a little disconcerting to wake up in such a pristine room, almost afraid to disturb anything.

Nevertheless, he was feeling considerably better than the night before. He was in a wide bed with a soft duvet, he'd taken medication to relieve the pain of his injuries and he was breathing so easily thanks to the advanced filtration system that when he finally withdrew the curtains, he found it hard to believe that beyond the glass was the same clogged atmosphere.

It had been twenty-four hours since he'd first arrived here at the hotel to meet Anders and for a while, he just let all the recessed thoughts drift through his mind, an eddy of images that whirled and twirled before he could fit them into place.

Three times now in his lifetime, he'd been present at massively disruptive events. The first, as a child, was amid the excesses of the Cultural Revolution. The second, as a young man, was when he ran from army bullets in the square to find refuge in the narrow *hutong*. And the third was just yesterday, when the military had taken over the Great Hall and an overly ambitious general had tried to take over the country.

He was still going over it all as he wrapped himself in the thick guest bathrobe before sitting down to his room service breakfast. In front of him, the official news channel was still broadcasting its own version of events when he received a call on his mobile.

He thought it might be his client, now in Tianjin, but it turned out to be his tenant, Liang, whom he hadn't seen since he left home the previous morning. He greeted her cheerfully but her voice seemed small and forlorn as she relayed the harrowing news that her roommate, Chen, was dead and that she was now staying with a friend. She also told him that she wouldn't be returning to the apartment for the foreseeable future except to pick up her things. Only then, as an afterthought, did she bother to add that she was sorry for the inconvenience.

After everything that had happened, this new shock hit Zhao especially hard. All he could do was mumble his condolences and then consider the depressing fact that neither of his tenants would be there anymore. Although they made the place seem more cramped, they were a nice young couple and they'd been welcome company. Just knowing they were there at night had made him feel less solitary, less adrift.

He finished the slow process of getting ready, gingerly changing the dressing on his split cheek and easing his clothes over the cumbersome chest bandages. Then he just stood for a while, gazing through the window at nothing at all. In theory, he had little to do today but his head was still in a state of upheaval and just like Liang, he really didn't feel like going back to the apartment right now.

That was when he had the notion.

Still parked downstairs in the hotel garage was the brand-new automobile of which he'd been so proud, making him realize that he didn't have to be alone. All he had to do was drive to Changchun, a mere six hundred miles distant, and by the end of this evening he could be kissing his wife and hugging his daughter. Thanks to his client, Anders, he now had enough cash in his wallet to buy whatever he needed for the journey, with even more to come on a regular basis, a steady income by virtue of the retainer.

Then another idea occurred to him, a thought that slowly brought the soft blur of moisture back to his eyes. But these tears weren't due to self-pity like yesterday morning in the car, the forlorn misery of loneliness and dashed hopes. These were more the tears of relief, because he now realized that he didn't actually have to sublet the room anymore. He could, in fact, afford to bring his family back down to the capital to stay with him on a permanent basis, just as they'd always planned. In his mind, he saw the joy on his family's faces as he told them the news, felt the warmth as they, too, began to understand that the long, long wait was finally over.

And with that happiest of all concepts floating before him, Zhao drove out from the hotel into the new yellow dawn and chose to forget, at least for a while, the crows that had cast such shadows. Once again, he'd managed to survive the day, as if to prove the enduring sagacity of his wife when she told him it's not strength of physique that keeps an ox steady, but the great size of his heart.

AFTERWORD

On March 19, 2012, the date on which this novel is set, there were indeed reports all over the globe of a possible coup d'état in Beijing. "Damaging coup rumors ricochet across China" headlined the BBC.

It happened after months of unusually vicious infighting by opposing factions of the Politburo. With several senior Party members having already been arrested, the climax seemed to arrive on this particular Monday with the sudden heavy presence of military activity around the government compound near Tiananmen Square. All at once, public speculation was rife, with each new theory transmitted instantly across the internet by foreign journalists and local bloggers alike.

Was it really a coup attempt? With hindsight, most commentators agree that it's doubtful but at the time, with the regime in a state of flux, such rumors appeared highly credible.

On a personal level, I'd just spent most of the previous decade working in China and while such melodramatic news grabbed the world's attention, my own fascination with that vast and complex land had come to mean so much more than the endless political machinations and struggles for control.

Perhaps what struck me the most on my travels was how many people had profound societal grievances and why they would choose to relate their problems to me, albeit in the strictest confidence.

While I cannot be sure, my impression was that they'd kept their problems bottled up for so long that they simply needed to speak to someone like myself—a discrete stranger with no local agenda, who not only understood the issues but also had the patience to listen and to empathize without judgment.

One acquaintance, for example, had no *hukou* for Beijing, just like my character Liang, and admitted to constant anxiety as a result. Another, like the architect, Sun, had seen a naive brother incarcerated for whistleblowing within a corrupt government department. Yet another was a lawyer, not unlike Feng, who was very much involved in the unofficial *weiquan* system to defend indvidual rights. And to my surprise, one even had the courage to whisper recollections of that notorious time in 1989—the events of June 4th—when the military opened fire on thousands of its own citizens.

In terms of personality, there were wide differences, too. Against all the odds, a few managed to maintain a certain quiet integrity, like my protagonist, Zhao. Others were more active, eager for peaceful protest whenever the opportunity presented itself, as demonstrated by the artist, Qian. However, in contrast to these rare individuals, there were far more who displayed the ruthless capitalism of the oligarch, Huang, the corrupt ideology of officials like Shui, or the bureaucratic acceptance of the acolyte, Yu.

In fact, all the characters featured are based on the most profound reality and while they're all composites in terms of age, gender, appearance and so forth—their personal safety requires that I do no less—I can assure readers that every backstory I describe, every anecdote I relate, is genuine and reliably sourced.

Over and above these human issues was the environmental degradation that I witnessed, including the noxious atmosphere that descended each year in early spring, when harsh desert grit mingled with the already thick pollutants, turning the skies bright yellow and causing that cancerous, throat-burning smog. I recall that whenever this occurred, there was such resentment that despite all the risks, it did occasionally manifest itself as open public protest.

In summary, I'd gathered a great deal of material on which to base a book, yet even with all this personal experience, it took considerable time for these multiple topics to coalesce and the written text to emerge.

To be honest, the problem was where to focus, whether it should be on the tragic environmental conditions, the potential for regime change, or the heartfelt stories of ordinary people. Each of these themes represented an essential facet of modern China and it was only after considerable thought that I developed the structure of a single, significant day on which I could bring all these diverse elements together.

The result became an amalgam of facts but in fictional form. In other words, while technically a novel, I believe this book can also be considered an insider's glimpse into this fascinating yet disconcerting society and its inhabitants.

In conclusion, I must offer several sincere acknowledgements. First, to my friend Dominic's sister, Mary, whose probing questions about China one evening inspired me to generate this concept. Also to my daughter, Janine, professor of English, who always provides such valuable feedback. Finally, my thanks and appreciation go as ever to my publisher, Jason, and his team at Grey Gecko for their efforts in bringing this work to fruition.

Leon Berger

About the Author

Leon now has over a dozen books published, including an Amazon #1 best-seller. Several have been translated for Europe, another for China, and two have won major international awards.

He has worked extensively across 5 continents, based in London, New York, Singapore and of course, Beijing, from where he journeyed all over China, getting to know the country, the people and the culture.

These days, he enjoys spending as much time as possible at home in Canada, where the long winter months provide enough peace and quiet for any project.

Connect with Leon

Email
lberger@videotron.ca

Website
www.lberger.ca

More from Leon Berger

books2read.com/ggp-horse

Horse

**Independent Publisher Book Awards
Silver Medalist**

*A heartwarming novel of friendship,
inspired by a true story.*

"Loved the story, couldn't stop reading."
—*Lionel Foster, horse owner, trainer, racer*

Amazon/Goodreads Reader Reviews:

"The story kept my attention throughout."
"Nice ending that I wouldn't have guessed
or expected."
"I love animal stories, and this was a good one."
"A gentle, heartwarming read."
"I read it in one day."

This charming chronicle tells the story of how a working horse finally gains his freedom.

The hero is a sturdy draft horse—old, eccentric and irritable. His name, suitably enough, is Groucho.

By day, he hauls a tourist carriage around the heritage streets of Montreal. By night, he goes home to a stable in a run-down, working-class district.

When his owner dies, Groucho feels the loss and is helped through it by the ancient stableman, Doyle, who is also set in his ways.

This story of friendship is about how they cope with each other, as well as the threat which endangers their entire way of life.

LUNCH WITH CHARLOTTE

The true saga of an extraordinary woman, set against the backdrop of history

"*Lunch With Charlotte* is one of the most powerful and moving books I've ever read. Tragedy, loss, heartache... and through it all, dignity and courage. This is a tale not to be missed."

— *Jason Kristopher, bestselling author of*
The Dying of the Light

books2read.com/charlotte

Every Friday for the last 25 years of her life, I had lunch with Charlotte and each week she told me more of her extraordinary story. To all appearances, she was a strong and dignified survivor, with old-world courtesies, a twinkling sense of humor, and a lilting Austrian syntax.

Yet deep within, she'd been scarred by a profound personal trauma. Finally, just before she died at the age of 91, she chose to entrust me with this profound secret and all at once I understood how it had affected her entire adult life.

NEW SECOND EDITION—NOW WITH PHOTO ARCHIVE!

"Mr. Berger transcribes a very emotional interpretation of the events of Mrs. Urban's life. I was moved by Mrs. Urban's ability to adapt to every situation thrown her way. Her life was not easy and continued to be a challenge. Lunch with Charlotte is an inspiring tale and very well worth a read."

—*Heather Robinson,* Readers' Favorite *5-star review*

Recommended Reading

books2read.com/hydra

The Year of the Hydra

Black Rain *meets* Fear & Loathing
in Las Vegas ... *with aliens.*

"A richly told, diagnosably insane, meandering-yet-captivating journey through everything good and bad about sex, drugs, and China—plus a wildly improbable tale about saving the world. In short, not to be missed."

—*H.C.H. Ritz, author of* **Absence of Mind**

Could a dark agenda be woven into the architecture of China's most sacred ancient temple? An agenda that only Julian Mancer is seeing? Or is Julian off his meds again? If the structure were in fact a doomsday device awaiting an astronomical tripwire—could Julian stop it?

Julian is determined to discover the answer, as soon as he concludes a far more pressing matter involving a sixteen-year-old girl with a most intriguing mutation ...

The Robin Hood Thief

In the face of death comes courage.

"Once again H.C.H. Ritz delivers a thoughtful action tale with the high-stakes urgency to keep the pages turning."

— *George Wright Padgett, bestselling author of* **Addleton Heights** *and* **Spindown**

Amazon Reader Reviews

books2read.com/
robin-hood

"H. C. H. Ritz writes a brilliant human drama overlaid on a dystopian landscape and carries us along moment by moment as the time-clock ticks down."

"Excellent writing, great characters and fantastic twist earned five stars. What if you had 45 days to live?"

Single mother Helen Dawson always wanted to be a hero. Now she's about to get her chance - but only because she's about to die. Given forty-five days to live, Helen sees this tragedy as a calling to do what others can't: turn her increasingly dystopian society upside down.

In a world ruled by economic injustice, Helen plans to steal from the rich and give to the poor—after providing for her teenage daughter. But with no thieving skills and no money, Helen will have to find the right allies and a ton of luck. Can she accomplish all the good she wants in the time that's left—and conquer the dangers to come?

The Robin Hood Thief is the third stand-alone novel by near-future science-fiction author H.C.H. Ritz. If you like fast-paced stories with a futuristic twist, you'll love this book. Begin this remarkable and exhilarating story today!

Support Indie Authors & Small Press

If you liked this book, please take a few moments to leave a review on your favorite website, even if it's only a line or two. Reviews make all the difference to indie authors and are one of the best ways you can help support our work.

Reviews on Amazon, GreyGeckoPress.com, GoodReads, or even on your own blog or website all help us to earn more readers just like you and keep publishing great indie books!

http://smarturl.it/review-harmony

Grey Gecko Press

Thank you for reading this book from Grey Gecko Press, an independent publishing company bringing you great books by your favorite new indie authors.

Be one of the first to hear about new releases from Grey Gecko: visit our website and sign up for our New Release or All-Access email lists. Don't worry: we hate spam, too. You'll only be notified when there's a new release, we'll never share your email with anyone for any reason, and you can unsubscribe at any time.

At our website you can purchase all our titles, including special and autographed editions, preorder upcoming books, and get other great special offers.

And don't forget: all our print editions come with the ebook free!

www.ingramcontent.com/pod-product-compliance
Lightning Source LLC
Chambersburg PA
CBHW030025200726
48283CB00012B/1017